Welcome to Harlequin's ~~great~~ **series, created by some** ~~of~~ **authors**

Twelve tales of heated romance and adventure—
guaranteed to turn your whole world upside down!

Travel to an Outback cattle station, experience the
glamour of the Gold Coast or visit the bright lights
of Sydney where you'll meet twelve engaging young
women, all feisty and all about to face their biggest
challenge yet...falling in love.

And it will take some very special women to tame
our heroes! Strong, rugged, often infuriating and
always irresistible, they're one hundred percent prime
Australian male: hard to get close to...but even
harder to forget!

The Wonder from Down Under:
where spirited women win the hearts of
Australia's most independent men.

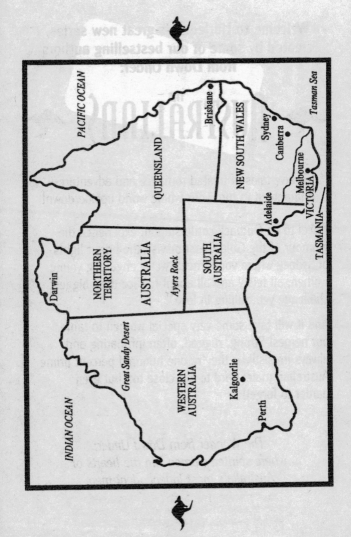

THE
AUSTRALIANS

PLAYBOY LOVER

Lindsay Armstrong

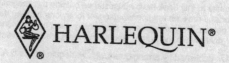

TORONTO • NEW YORK • LONDON
AMSTERDAM • PARIS • SYDNEY • HAMBURG
STOCKHOLM • ATHENS • TOKYO • MILAN • MADRID
PRAGUE • WARSAW • BUDAPEST • AUCKLAND

ISBN 0-373-82575-7

PLAYBOY LOVER

First North American Publication 1998.

Copyright © 1996 by Lindsay Armstrong.

This edition published by arrangement with Harlequin Books S.A.

® and TM are trademarks of the publisher. Trademarks indicated with ® are registered in the United States Patent and Trademark Office, the Canadian Trade Marks Office and in other countries.

Printed in U.S.A.

Lindsay Armstrong lives in Australia with her New Zealand-born husband and five children. They have lived in nearly every state of Australia and tried their hand at some unusual, for them, occupations, such as farming and horse-training—all grist to the mill for a writer! Lindsay started writing romances when their youngest child began school and she was left feeling at a loose end. She is still doing it and loving it.

CHAPTER ONE

'YOU'RE...gorgeous.'

Dominique Lindwall didn't reply. Instead she took several ragged breaths and closed her eyes while the man holding her continued to kiss her throat and bare shoulders. And she tried dimly to concentrate on the fact that she knew him only by his first name, that he was the kind of man she normally avoided like the plague...

Yet here she was, on a moon-washed white terrace overlooking the Southport Broadwater and a forest of yacht masts, being more and more intimately embraced by this man whom she'd met only an hour or so earlier at a party that she'd been in two minds about attending anyway.

He was an undeniably attractive man, who had cut a swathe through the party on his arrival—late—by virtue of his height, his broad shoulders and lean hips, his thick fair hair and a pair of rather remarkable blue eyes that were both worldly and indifferent.

In fact, Dominique doubted that any woman guest had not felt the impact of him, and even she, who was inured to wildly attractive men, or so she'd thought, had felt a frisson before deliberately switching those kinds of thoughts off.

But after a few words with their hostess he had crossed directly to her side, introduced himself, claimed her for a dance and somehow it had all led on from there.

They hadn't talked much but they'd danced together for nearly an hour and their steps had fitted perfectly. What was more, their bodies had fitted well as they'd moved together—although when this had struck her she'd covered it with an ironic little glance up at him from her cool green eyes, only to receive a quizzical look in reply. He'd continued to guide her with his slim, strong hands on her hips, and had managed to engender in her the feeling that the fine material of her sleek black dress might as well have been non-existent.

That was when she'd been reluctantly shaken out of her own, deliberate indifference and had wondered who he was.

The party was a dinner dance celebrating the birthday of a friend, who had taken over a restaurant in the Marina Mirage complex for the occasion.

Dominique had sighed inwardly on arrival, alone, to see the usual throng that surrounded Gayle Gyngell, wildly successful dress designer, whose birthday it was. The 'usual throng' sometimes seemed to her to *exist* on champagne and any excuse for a party, and amongst the 'usual throng' the chief topics of conversation were clothes and hairdressers or cars and golf, which five-star resort to choose for one's next holiday and whether one should wait or sell one's blue-chip investments.

'Look, Dom, do come!' Gayle had pleaded over the phone. 'You can't hide away for ever now you and Bryce have split up. It's been months and months anyway—it looks as if you've gone into mourning or something like that! And if you're afraid of bumping into him, he has *not* been invited.'

'I haven't and I'm not,' Dominique had replied shortly.

'Then prove it, darling. Believe me, as one of your

oldest friends—' they'd been at the same school together throughout their school years '—I know you
need to get out and about again! Besides which, there
are some fascinating people coming.'

Yet it was the same old throng, she'd thought, and
had damned herself for being taunted into coming. Until, that was, this man who was kissing her now had
appeared at her side and said simply, 'Hi, I'm Rory. I
believe you're Dominique—would you dance with me?'

Why did I accept? she asked herself now, with a
sense of disbelief. Because I was tired of pretending to
be a bright, talkative party animal? Because I lacked an
escort? Because Gayle had me firmly fixed in her sights
and would not have stopped at hauling me back if I'd
tried to slip away? Or because it was a challenge, a
gauntlet thrown down, a man who was so very sure of
himself, a man I could prove something to—that he
wasn't going to bowl *me* over...?

She winced inwardly as she remembered how she'd
answered him with a simple yes but with an undertone
of weariness and a complete lack of interest.

Then she'd made her discovery of how well they
went together and had encountered that quizzical look,
had realised that he had a deep, beautifully modulated
voice and spoke in a cultured manner. She'd also made
the discovery that his sense of rhythm matched hers,
that he was very light on his feet and that he had beautiful hands...

I must be mad, she'd thought, not risking a second
glance into those quizzical blue eyes.

That had been when he'd said, 'Would you like to
talk, Dominique? Or should we just dance?'

She had looked up involuntarily then and seen an
amused query in his eyes, so she'd shrugged as if it

hadn't mattered to her what they did and murmured, 'I'm tired of talking, but if you really—'

'Not at all,' he'd cut in, and moved his hands on her hips. 'Well, may I say that your dress becomes you beautifully?' And he'd let his gaze drift down her body, clothed in one of Gayle's creations—a long, clinging black silk jersey shift with shoestring straps and no adornment other than the strand of real pearls she wore.

Her long, naturally curly fair hair with golden highlights was loose and tucked behind her ears to reveal matching pearl studs. She wore no rings, no bracelets, not even a watch, but she had a tiny velvet purse looped around one wrist with the barest essentials in it: her car keys, a hanky, lipstick and a fifty-dollar note.

'It must have something to do with your exquisite skin,' he'd continued, and moved those beautiful hands up to the bare skin of her upper arms. 'It needs very little ornamentation.'

Dominique had raised an eyebrow as if to say that she'd heard it all before and he'd laughed quietly and appeared entirely unabashed—and that had been when she'd decided that there was something very grown-up about Mr Rory whoever-he-was, yet it still didn't interest her in the slightest. And she'd beamed a single glance of green-eyed contempt up at him but had danced on.

She would think, the next day, that it was a pity that the music had slowed then and become languorous and dreamy—the kind of music you either danced intimately to or made you leave the floor.

She would wonder why on earth she hadn't left the floor, and what strange power a strange man had possessed over her so that she'd been caught up in the feel of his arms around her, his hard-honed, beautifully proportioned body against hers. Or, she would wonder, could she blame it on the music? A reluctance to return to the fray? An inner ache of loneliness that had been with her for months? Had she quite simply needed a man? It wouldn't be a pleasant thought.

Yet the fact was that when the band had finally taken a break, he'd taken her hand and led her through the crowd out onto the deserted terrace, out of sight, and had taken her straight back into his arms...

'Dominique?'

'Mr...Rory,' she said raggedly, 'no more. Not here... I mean...'

'I agree,' he said deeply and quietly, but kissed her swollen lips once again, although lightly this time, and ran his hand over the riotous curls of her hair. 'Will you come with me?'

'Well, I need to get away,' she said a little desperately as she realised that one of her shoestring straps had broken when he'd pushed it aside to kiss the hollow of her shoulder.

'It's just across the road. Come.' He released her and took her hand, and added as she tensed, 'We don't have to go back inside.'

So she followed him down the outside stairs; she could think of nothing else to do and held up her dress with the other hand so as not to trip as she tried to keep up with his long strides. But he slowed once they were in the main concourse—and she started to come to her senses.

She pulled her hand free and stopped. She ran her fingers through her hair, felt for her broken strap and looked up into his blue eyes. '*Where?*'

'I'm staying at the Sheraton Mirage, just across the road. Dominique—'

'No!' she said hoarsely. 'I'm not that kind of... No, we don't even know each other!'

Their gazes locked, then his drifted down to the upper curve of her breast, exposed by the broken strap, and he said, 'I thought we were getting to know each other rather well.'

A tide of colour burnt her cheeks but he went on, 'I quite thought that's how you preferred to—get to know men, Dominique.'

'How did you know my name?' she whispered, her green eyes wide and horrified.

He smiled twistedly. 'Has it just occurred to you? I asked, that's all.'

'Why?'

'I liked the look of you.'

She swallowed.

'I liked the way you moved, the way you looked—so bored and proud, yet with that stunning body—well, pretty much on display,' he said with soft mockery. 'I wondered what it would take to make you come alive. I wasn't far wrong either.'

'What do you mean?'

'You certainly came alive for a while in my arms on the terrace,' he said with a wryly lifted eyebrow. 'I didn't hear one protestation of maidenly outrage at all. Which is why this is a bit of a surprise, I guess, Dominique.'

'You...' Dominique spat the word, then raised her hand and slapped him soundly and spun on her heel to run away as fast as she could.

'I gather we're not in a good mood this morning.'

Dominique eyed her secretary, dumped a folder unceremoniously on her desk and sat down behind it. 'You gather right.'

'Why?' Sally Henderson, who reminded Dominique of a bright, inquisitive, middle-aged bird at times, perched herself on the corner of the desk.

'Why would I be?' Dominique retorted, and rubbed the back of her neck. 'You must know how tiresome these meetings are. Talk about rallying the troops!'

'Is that what he's on about again?' Sally said, referring to the senior partner of the prestigious accounting firm that they both worked for, Dominique as a specialist taxation consultant.

'Yes,' Dominique said shortly. '"Don't lose any accounts on pain of death" kind of thing.' She looked about her cluttered desk. 'I have so many accounts I don't know where to begin!'

'That's because you've taken over some from old Smithy, which is really a feather in your cap,' Sally consoled her. 'I mean, you're only twenty-seven but one could say with some honesty that you're a rising star in this here firm, Miss Lindwall.'

'At the moment I'm only overworked and underpaid—well—' Dominique grimaced '—that's not quite true.'

'I should think not,' Sally said primly, eyeing the lovely thyme-green linen suit that Dominique wore, with its wide-shouldered long jacket and short skirt over a black silk blouse, and the fine black stockings and black suede pumps. 'Not many of us can afford to wear Gayle Gyngell.'

Dominique closed her eyes involuntarily but said automatically, 'How many times do I have to tell you, Sal? I get a discount. I know—' she held up a hand '—I know I could probably afford them anyway, before you charge me with that too, but we've known each other for as long as I can remember. I used to help her sew up her first creations when we were about twelve.'

'Uh-huh. You didn't have a late night by any chance?'

Dominique sat back warily. 'What makes you say that?'

'You look a little peaked, that's all. Faint shadows under your eyes,' Sally said critically. 'Of course, these meetings are even harder to take under those circumstances.'

'Go away, Sally, will you?' Dominique said wearily. 'No—hang on; we better go through my diary first.'

'Right! Then I'll bring you a nice, reviving cup of coffee. Let's see…at twelve o'clock you have Emory Jones—'

'Never heard of him.'

'That's because he was old Smithy's client, and a *big* one,' Sally said significantly. 'One of the ones it wouldn't be wise to lose, in other words. The family has been with the firm since time immemorial.'

'And today of all days,' Dominique muttered. 'Go on.'

Sally did, and finally left, assuring her again that she would return with coffee.

Dominique eyed the closing door balefully, then sat back and sighed. The truth was that she had hardly slept, and she had barely half an hour to acquaint herself with the taxation concerns of one Emory Jones. Then her phone rang and it was Gayle.

'Darling, I didn't see you leave last night! Were you all right?'

'Fine,' Dominique said brightly, but felt her cheeks starting to burn. 'It was a lovely party, Gay.'

'What did you think of Rory? Saw you two dancing.'

Dominique swallowed. 'He was...interesting!'

'He sure is. Didn't get a chance to tell you about him; actually it was only coincidence he was there! I bumped into him unexpectedly yesterday afternoon—apparently he's down for a few days—and I invited him on the *spot*. Let me tell you, Dom, Rory is—'

'Gayle, I'm terribly sorry but I'm with a client,' Dominique interrupted a little desperately and with a lie. 'Can I get back to you?'

'Of course!' But it was virtually impossible to halt Gayle when she was in full spate. 'So you see, old thing, life after Bryce is possible; what did I tell you? And *Rory* is just the one—'

'Bye, Gayle!' Dominique put the phone down and came to the decision that although she didn't know how she would achieve it she would definitely be avoiding one of her best friends for a time. I just can't believe I did it, she thought, and closed her eyes painfully.

So it was a welcome interruption after all when Sally returned with the coffee, and Dominique admonished herself as she drank it to concentrate on business, and in particular on the business of Emory Jones, whoever he was.

He was probably as dry and desiccated as most of old Smithy's clients had turned out to be, she mused, although her eyes widened as she flicked through a thick file. The assets listed to one Emory Jones were very impressive—two cattle stations, a ceramics factory, a chain of hardware stores, a *gold* mine...

Dominique blinked a couple of times and read on until she was interrupted by the fire alarm, which caused her to frown impatiently and mutter beneath her breath. The firm of Conrod, Whitney & Smith, Chartered

Accountants, had recently moved to offices in a new building, and while they were spacious, impressive and luxurious, and overlooked the Nerang River as it wound behind Suffers Paradise, one of the teething problems of the building was an erratic fire alarm that went off for no reason at all.

Sally poked her head round the door. 'I think it's only a false alarm but I'll check—if not I'll come back and get you.'

'Thanks,' Dominique said wryly. 'Heaven knows what will happen if we get a real fire one day.'

Sally laughed and departed, and Dominique forced herself to concentrate once again. Thus it was that when there was a light knock on her door she didn't even raise her head as she called the person to come in.

But when she did lift her head at last she found that it wasn't Sally; it was the man she knew only as Rory, casually dressed in jeans and a black shirt today but just as devastatingly impressive, and with a familiar, quizzical glint in his blue eyes as though chasing a look of surprise...

If he was surprised Dominique was speechless for a long moment as their gazes locked. Then she stood up carefully, held onto the back of her chair and said tautly, 'Now look here, I have not the slightest desire to see you again; you have no right to turn up here, so will you please go away?'

'Uh—' his lips moved into a sweet but mocking little smile '—unfortunately I do have a right to be here, Dominique, so—'

'No, you don't!' she broke in fiercely. 'I suppose you've been onto Gayle; well, *she* had no right to tell you where I worked and—and I refuse to be hounded, so if you don't go of your own accord I will have you escorted from the building, Mr...?'

'Jones,' he supplied. 'We never did get around to trading surnames, did we?' And for a moment that worldly indifference was there in his eyes again, and for some reason it caused her to shiver inwardly.

But she got angry again almost immediately. 'Mr *Jones*, then!' she said, with her own eyes a narrowed, cold green, but then they widened and her lips parted as she also noticed for the first time that he carried a folder of papers. 'You don't mean—?'

Sally hopped into the room at this point. 'It *was* another false alarm— Oh, you must be Mr Emory Jones. I'm sorry I wasn't here to greet you so I could do my little spiel, but the wretched fire alarm—well, never mind, I'll do it now! Miss Lindwall, may I introduce Mr Emory Jones, who was a very valued client of our recently retired partner Mr Lancelot Smith? Mr Jones— Miss Lindwall, who will be taking care of all your needs now. Can I get you some coffee?'

'No, thank you,' Emory Jones said with obviously suppressed laughter. 'I think I'd like to get right down to—having my needs taken care of by Miss Lindwall. So you've taken over from old Smithy, Dominique. Congratulations!' And he held out his hand.

Dominique stared at it transfixed, and Sally, shaken out of her super-secretary mode, said in surprise, 'You two know each other?'

'We do indeed,' Emory Jones murmured. 'Quite intimately, as it happens. Don't we, Dominique?'

She drew a deep breath and shook his hand briefly. 'Please sit down. Mr Jones is exaggerating, Sally,' she said in a brisk, businesslike voice. 'And, even if he wouldn't, I'd like another cup of coffee, please.'

'Will do,' Sally murmured, but in a mystified way, and withdrew.

'So—' Dominique sat down herself and clasped her hands on the desk '—I'm afraid I haven't had a lot of time to study your tax situation, Mr Jones; it looks rather complex but—'

'Do you really think this is going to work, Dominique?' Emory Jones queried, sprawling out in a chair and capturing her gaze with a lot of amusement in his blue eyes. 'I mean,' he went on to explain politely as she swallowed, 'can we simply ignore what happened last night? It doesn't seem very honest, does it?' He raised an eyebrow at her.

'Are you that qualified to preach honesty?' she retorted. 'One minute you're Rory, then you're Emory—'

'Rory is the diminutive of Emory, as Bill is to William, etcetera, Dominique—didn't you know?'

'Obviously not.' She glared at him. 'I've never met an Emory before.'

'One lives and learns,' he murmured. 'For example, I don't think I've ever met a chartered accountant who looks like you. Certainly a very far cry from old Smithy.' He smiled. 'It's the last profession I would have thought suited you, so—'

'Yes, well, we do know what profession you had me marked down for, Mr Jones,' Dominique said acidly, and added, 'I have to tell you it gives me a great deal of satisfaction to prove you wrong.'

His eyes narrowed. 'There's no law that says you can't be both.'

Dominique coloured faintly but forced herself to lean back and say coolly, 'If you're basing this attack on what happened last night, isn't it a slight case of the pot calling the kettle black?'

'The thing is,' he said, unperturbed, linking his slim, strong hands together, 'I'm not altogether sure what *did* happen last night. It was such a purely unspoken yet *vividly* sensual affair, wasn't it?' His eyes mocked her.

Dominique bit her lip then smiled frostily, and with irony. 'Just like ships passing in the night, Mr Jones! I really think we'll have to leave it there—if for no other reason than because I'm literally snowed under with work. It will take me a few weeks to prepare your personal income-tax assessment, so could we start to go through it now?'

She pulled a pad towards her and picked up a pen, and breathed a sigh of relief as Sally entered with another cup of coffee.

Her relief was short-lived as Emory Jones smiled beguilingly at Sally and said, 'Would it be possible to get Frank Conrod on the phone for me? I always have a word with him when I'm in town. He and my father were great friends.'

Sally didn't even look at Dominique for confirmation. She picked up the phone and after a couple of moments handed it to him. 'Mr Conrod, Mr Jones.'

Dominique tightened her mouth and sat back with elaborate patience as she swung her pen in her fingers. Sally again withdrew, but this time after intercepting a laser-like look from Dominique and mouthing with injured innocence, Did I do something wrong?

And Emory Jones said genially down the line, 'Frank! How are you?'

Dominique swivelled her chair round to face the window and the view of the river as the conversation progressed, then stiffened and listened incredulously.

'Frank, old man,' Emory Jones drawled into the phone, 'there is one thing you could help me with. You know I always used to take Lancelot out to lunch? Yep! Quite an institution it was. Well, I was wondering whether you could persuade Miss Lindwall that it's perfectly all right for her to have lunch with me? She seems to think she's too busy.'

Dominique swivelled back furiously to find him offering the phone to her. 'Your boss,' he said gently.

'Of all the...' Dominique closed her eyes then took the phone. 'Yes, Mr Conrod. Well, I am exceedingly busy, as you yourself know, what with Mr Smith's clients on top of my own... I see. Yes. Yes, indeed. No, of course not.' She put the phone down and raised her eyes to meet Emory Jones's.

'It's on?' he queried lightly.

'It's on. What a coward you are, Mr Jones,' she said scathingly.

He laughed softly. 'Needs must when the devil drives, Miss Lindwall. Shall we go? It's twelve-thirty now—rather a good time to break for lunch, don't you agree?'

'A Caesar salad? Is that all? Come, Miss Lindwall, you really don't need to cut off your nose to spite your face—the lobster here at Grumpy's is marvellous.'

Grumpy's Wharf Restaurant, unfortunately, was upstairs in the Mariner's Cove complex, just next door to the Marina Mirage, so the view from their table outside on the deck was not a lot different from the view that Dominique had witnessed last night from a terrace that she would dearly have loved to be able to forget. The only real difference was that sunlight instead of moonlight played on the Broadwater.

Is this deliberate? she wondered as she sipped mineral

water and cast Emory Jones a dark little look from beneath her lashes— Of course it is!

'I agree with you,' she said drily. 'The lobster is marvellous here, but I'm not in the habit of eating large lunches.'

'Or drinking alcohol at lunchtime.'

She raised her mineral water to him ironically. 'No.'

'In other words,' he said, 'you're determined to make this as painful an exercise as you can. Do you always hate the men who arouse you, Dominique?'

CHAPTER TWO

A BLAZE of anger lit her eyes as she glanced at Emory Jones briefly and said equally briefly, 'No.'

'Then why do you hate me so much?'

Dominique took a deep breath that caused her nostrils to flare, and rearranged her cutlery at perfect right angles to the edge of the table. Then she sipped some more mineral water before she finally felt controlled enough to look across at him again. 'Look, it was a momentary aberration that I can't entirely explain. It—' she gestured frustratedly '—was just one of those things.'

'No, it wasn't,' he countered coolly. 'We—clicked, Dominique, whether you care to admit it or not. Unless you prefer me to go back to my earlier assumption that you're one of those voracious women who can't resist a one-night stand? But something happened to make you change your mind—last night, that is. Are you trying to reform?' he queried gravely.

'I could accuse *you* of that—one-night stands and so on,' she said tautly. 'Excepting that you are obviously *not* trying to reform.'

'You could,' he drawled, 'but in my case it was much simpler. I saw you across the room, I was immediately, completely…struck, and impelled to get to know you better. *Are* you trying to reform?' he repeated.

'Don't say that to me again,' she retorted dangerously. 'I'm liable to start throwing things.'

He laughed softly, but his eyes were cool, mocking

22

and very blue. And his reply was forced to wait as their meals arrived—his a tantalising lobster mornay.

The wine waiter descended on them at the same time, flourishing a bottle of Heggies Rhine Riesling, whereupon Emory Jones told him that his guest had changed her mind and would partake of a glass of wine after all.

Dominique flashed him another furious look but discovered that, truth be told, she was beginning to feel as if she needed it.

'That's better,' he said quietly when they'd both sipped some wine. 'You were starting to look a bit pale around the gills, Miss Lindwall. Do start; not that a salad is going to put much fortification into you.'

Dominique gazed down at her despised salad, took another sip of wine and said suddenly, 'I don't know why I did it, Mr Jones. I've…' she paused '…tried to have things out with myself, if it's any consolation to you. And if it's any further consolation to you I was quite horrified to think I could have…gone to those lengths with a man I didn't know.

'I've asked myself whether it was the music, whether I was bored with a party I didn't particularly want to go to, in a mood that wasn't particularly—that wasn't festive in the slightest, to be honest. I've even asked myself whether I simply needed a man, which is a *particularly* humiliating thing to wonder about oneself.'

She stopped but he said nothing, only gazed at her attentively. 'And I guess I should apologise to you for building up your expectations the way I may have, only to…' She hesitated and sought for words.

'Only to resort to the old slap-in-the-face routine?' he suggested wickedly.

She flushed but said baldly, 'Yes. So there you are. Does that explain why I could have died when you walked into my office this morning and why it's extremely embarrassing to be here with you now? I hope so, because it's the truth.'

He took up a forkful of steaming lobster coated in melted cheese and gazed at it thoughtfully for a moment, then said, raising his eyes to hers, 'You must surely have been a little attracted to me?' And popped the forkful into his mouth with appreciation.

'If you must know—' Dominique ate a piece of lettuce leaf and a crouton '—my first impression of you was that you were far too sure of yourself to be—at all likeable.'

He grinned. 'I did get that impression, as a matter of fact—why did you accept?'

'I told you, I was bored,' she said wearily.

'Well, what about second impressions?'

'Look, I think I'm going to fall back on the standard "no comment" routine, Mr Jones—'

'Rory. All my friends call me that—and, before you say a word, even old Smithy used to call me that—and the "no comment" routine really won't do, Dominique. It places your whole explanation at risk, you see.'

'No, I don't see!' she said, irritably and unwisely.

'Put it this way, then: even if it's the music, or whatever, do you usually go around kissing men who don't appeal to you at all?'

Dominique stared at him with her mouth set into a hard line, but could think of nothing to say.

'On the other hand,' he went on, 'if you have a grudge against men, if you have cause to be bitter about one man in particular or the whole species in general but you couldn't quite resist the spontaneous magic that occurred between us last night—now, that would make much more sense. I mean, more sense for a girl who was genuinely horrified at what she'd done, as you say you were.'

Dominique sighed. 'I think it might be simpler if you just think what you like about me, Mr...Rory.' She smiled a meaningless, give-nothing-away smile and concentrated on her salad.

After a moment he went back to eating his lobster, but that wasn't, she discovered, because he'd withdrawn his offensive. When he'd finished, he wiped his mouth with his napkin and said meditatively, 'You might as well tell me who he was and what happened, Dominique.'

'*No*... That is—' Dominique tried to backtrack hastily '—this is ridiculous!'

Rory Jones raised a lazy eyebrow. 'I can always ask our mutual friend, Gayle. It was she who told me your name. She also gave me a bit of advice.'

'What?' Dominique demanded through her teeth.

'She said, ''Go for it, Rory; she needs someone like you.'' All of which, including the way you are, indicates to me that your—walk through the jungle of love has been a treacherous experience to date.'

Dominique said something beneath her breath then added quite clearly, 'Well, you're both wrong. Personally I think the last person I need is someone like you. I know absolutely nothing about you—'

'Other than that you like me dancing with you, kissing and holding you, but go on.'

'Other than that you have a complicated personal income-tax situation, Mr Jones,' Dominique said deliberately.

'Ah, that!' he responded genially, but with devilish amusement dancing in his eyes. 'Now you've put me in mind of it, Dominique, so I do.' And he narrowed

his eyes and added thoughtfully, 'It would be a pity if
you were to lose my…complicated personal income-tax
situation, Dominique, wouldn't it?'

'What do you mean?'

'I don't think Frank Conrod would take too kindly to
me going somewhere else,' he mused gently.

Her green eyes widened in sudden comprehension.
'You wouldn't!'

'I don't know what I might do unless you agree to
have dinner with me—not tonight, unfortunately, but
tomorrow night.'

'That's blackmail,' she said in a stunned voice.

'I know,' he agreed, coolly and casually.

Dominique put a hand to her brow uncertainly.

'Look, why don't you just do it?' Rory Jones said
with a sudden undertone of rough impatience. 'I'm not
a monster, I didn't force you in any way last night and
you're mad if you think you can bury that beautiful
body away because some man did the wrong thing by
you. You certainly look as if you should have more
spunk than that.'

Dominique took her hand away. 'All right,' she said
in a clipped voice. 'Just bear this in mind, Rory Jones.
It's taken me a lot of hard work to get where I am with
Conrod, Whitney & Smith, and I'm not about to jeopardise it over you. All the same there's a limit—don't
plan on blackmailing me any further, in other words.
And, if you don't mind, there are quite a few things I
need to know to be able to prepare your tax return—'

'I left it all on your desk,' he interrupted. 'I have
another appointment at two, but if there's anything that
needs clarifying you can ring me at the Mirage. I'll pick
you up tomorrow night at about—seven?' He raised an
eyebrow at her.

'No, thank you. I'll meet you wherever it is we're dining,' she replied evenly.

'Well, where would you like to go?'

'I don't care in the slightest.'

He grinned. 'I see. Uh...let's make it somewhere classy. I rather like you in evening wear. Let's make it Horizons at the Mirage.' He looked at her blandly. 'That would be very convenient for me.'

'No, I've got a better idea; let's make it casual at the Terraces—same hotel, different venue but just as convenient for you. That's my last offer.'

'OK,' he said with a charming smile. 'That'll do. I'll make the booking. I suppose you're all hepped up on lettuce leaves now and ready to get back to work? Would you mind if I called you a taxi, Dominique?'

'I'd be delighted,' she murmured. They'd come in his huge, powerful, latest model Land Rover, which she'd found quite a test of her skirt simply to climb into, amongst other things.

'You're so gracious,' he commented.

'You don't know the half of it yet, buddy,' she murmured.

'Obviously,' he said wryly. 'Unfortunately, if this is some kind of strategy—on your part, I mean—it only leads me to want to know more...'

When she got home that evening after working late, Dominique showered, changed into a yellow robe, made herself something to eat then roamed her apartment for about ten minutes.

She lived in a luxury two-bedroomed apartment on the fifteenth floor of a block that overlooked the Broadwater about fifteen minutes north of the Sheraton and Marina Mirage.

Her parents had been killed in a car accident a couple of years previously, and as their only child she'd inherited a not insubstantial estate and didn't actually have to work for a living.

She'd furnished the apartment in shades of grey and lemon with touches of dusky pink, and it was cool, comfortable and a pleasant haven.

She had a wonderful view too, over the narrow green sliver of South Stradbroke Island to the Pacific Ocean beyond. It gave her no pleasure at all this evening, however, and finally she picked up the phone and dialled.

'Gayle—'

'Dom! I quite thought you were fobbing me off this morning,' Gayle Gyngell said reproachfully down the line.

Dominique winced and sat down beside her telephone table. 'Sorry, Gayle. I—was busy. Uh…where were we?'

'Talking about Rory,' Gayle said in a much happier voice.

'Oh, yes; tell me a bit about him,' Dominique said reluctantly, but unable to help herself.

'Didn't he tell you anything about himself?'

Dominique moved a silver-framed miniature of her mother on the beautifully inlaid surface of the table. 'Not a lot, no.'

'Well, then,' Gayle said comfortably, 'he's wildly rich, for one thing. There are cattle stations and gold mines—you name it, the Jones family is into it.'

'How come I haven't heard of them?' Dominique asked with a frown.

'Oh, they're *very* discreet, darling. Few people have probably; it's that kind of old money.'

'How did you meet him, then, Gay?'

'Well, I first met him years ago, but I only really got to know him after I designed his sister's wedding dress; that was about four years ago and it was a big coup for me. I got an awful lot of custom out of it—'

'Hang on—not that silver strapless one?'

'None other.' Gayle laughed. 'His sister and I are of one mind when it comes to breaking some traditions. You didn't like it, did you, Dom? I must say it was very different to your dress…um…'

'Yes. So?' Dominique said coolly.

'Sorry, love. Well, I got to know him better, went out with him a few times, had an absolute ball but—' Gayle sighed theatrically '—all I managed to achieve was to stay friends of a kind.'

'How so?'

'Darling, these things just happen; either you're soul mates or you're mates of another kind.'

'So you didn't…?' Dominique bit her lip.

'Didn't sleep with him, no. I wasn't asked.'

'You did say you had a ball.'

'Oh, yes! What I meant was, you never knew when he was going to pick you up with a group of friends in a helicopter and take you across the border for lunch or—that kind of thing.'

'I see.'

'Dom, you could do with a bit of that,' Gayle said earnestly. 'After Bryce—'

'Has he ever been married?' Dominique cut in swiftly.

'Rory? Nope. To be honest, I don't know whether he'd be too comfortable to be married to. He's crazy in some respects—he can't sit still, he loves exploring and mountaineering, skiing, doing all sorts of wild and wonderful things—he should have been born a century earlier, I reckon. But there's no doubt he has women lying down in the aisles for him; I guess that was pretty obvious, even to you, Dom.'

Dominique winced and said bleakly, 'Yes.' But she added with more spirit, 'Not that that makes him—well, likeable.' She heard her voice echoed in her mind with another wince.

There was a pause, then Gayle said, 'Dominique, you are still wrapped up in that bastard Bryce, aren't you? You *must* be not to... Mind you, I saw you and Rory dancing—'

Dominique laughed hollowly. 'I must have been mad.'

'So what's the state of play?' Gayle asked rather carefully.

'Dinner tomorrow night, that's all. Gay, if he gets in touch with you could you...would you remember we've been friends a lot longer than you and Rory Jones?'

'What's that supposed to mean?'

'Don't tell him anything about me. Please.'

'All right, but why?'

'I just—he's not my cup of tea, that's all. I *was* a bit miserable and lonely last night and he, well— I know, I know! I'll get over it, but Rory Jones is *not* the man to help me do it.'

'Why are you having dinner with him, then?' Gayle enquired pointedly.

'Because he blackmailed me into it,' Dominique said coldly. 'As it turns out, he's one of the clients I inherited from the partner who retired recently, and—'

'Oho!' Gayle marvelled. 'So that's how the milk got into the coconut.'

'Gay, please!'

'Dearest,' Gayle said soulfully, 'have we not been

friends since we were five? Of course I won't do anything against your wishes. But I must say this—if Rory
Jones *wants* you, there may not be an awful lot you can
do about it.'

Oh, yes, there is, Dominique was still saying to herself
as she crossed the impressive marble and gold foyer of
the Sheraton Mirage towards the Terraces the following
evening—oh, yes there is!

She was wearing an emerald-green silk blouse,
sparsely patterned with big white chrysanthemums,
tucked into emerald green linen trousers with a narrow
bronze belt and bronze shoes. Her curly hair was tied
back loosely tonight and her pale golden skin—so de-
scribed once by a man whom she was doing her best to
forget—wore the minimum of make-up.

She had naturally thick, curved eyebrows that she
never plucked, and a generous mouth, and as she
walked through a few men stopped to look at her—
something she took no notice of. She was five feet six
and walked lithely and with the kind of confidence that
good posture training gave one. She was not, however,
feeling all that confident, despite the words she was re-
peating to herself.

The *maître d'* greeted her, and when she told him
who she was joining became even more effusive as he
led her to a table where Emory Jones sat waiting for
her. And for a long moment they stared into each
other's eyes, before he stood up courteously.

'You came,' he said at last, when she'd been seated.

'Didn't you expect me to?' she replied with a cool
arch of an eyebrow.

'I wondered, that's all. Poison?'

'I beg your pardon—? Oh. Yes, I'm wearing Poison, Mr Jones. How very perceptive of you.'

'Did you think I was referring to your state of mind, Dominique?' His eyes glinted devilishly.

She let her gaze drift coolly over him. He had on a big white, well-pressed thick cotton shirt with button-down patch pockets and a pair of grey denim trousers, and his fair hair was brushed and shining. 'Will I do?' he murmured, following her gaze. Then he looked back up into her eyes.

Since, yet again, he was obviously the most compelling man in the restaurant, Dominique for some reason found what he'd said amusing, and she couldn't help smiling wryly.

'Oh, now,' he immediately said softly, 'you should do that more often, Dominique. It's like sunshine. What did I say that was so funny, though?'

She looked away. 'Nothing.'

'Well—what are you going to have to eat this evening? You've no excuse for a salad tonight.'

'I'll have…smoked salmon and a…and a fillet steak, thank you.'

'That's my girl,' he said, and ordered for them both. 'Now that's done,' he added comfortably, 'why don't you tell me a bit about yourself? How you got into accounting, for example.'

Dominique thought for a moment. 'I think I inherited my father's passion for figures, for order and rationality, analysis and assessment and thoroughness.'

'Different people find different things fascinating,' he commented.

'What do you find fascinating?' Dominique queried.

'Apart from you?' He grimaced. 'A lot of things. So you're *clever*, Dominique. As well as cool and rational and career-minded. Has that ever been a problem?' He stared at her with his head to one side and once again he was that worldly, indifferent man who had thrown down a gauntlet to her with such disastrous consequences.

'What do you mean?' she said tartly.

'With men?'

She opened her mouth, closed it, then said neutrally, 'Sometimes.'

His eyes glinted with humour. 'This is like pulling teeth.'

She coloured faintly but said, 'We could always talk about the weather.'

'We could, but let's try another tack. Do you like to travel?'

'Yes, I do. Very much. I have a holiday planned to Malaysia this year, in about six weeks—always assuming I can get the time off,' she said ruefully. 'And I hope to be able to include some of the more out of the way places such as Sarawak, Kota Baharu, and there's an island called Rawa I've heard of—'

'Lovely!'

'You've been there?'

'Yes,' he said. 'It's very simple, though. Mostly two-roomed huts and not on the tourist track exactly. In fact it's usually frequented by Singaporeans getting away from all that. But it's a beautiful island.'

Dominique sat forward with her chin in her hand. 'How do you actually get there? My travel agent is a bit mystified.'

'We drove to Mersing. We hired a car in Kota Baharu and drove right down the east coast, which is considerably less populated than the west, through Kuala

Terengganu, Cherrating, Kuantan and so on. Then we left the car on the mainland and took the ferry across.'

'So there's a regular ferry service?'

'Uh-huh, but the times vary according to the tide. You have to traverse this rather shallow estuary to get out to sea. I'll never forget my first sight of the jetty on Rawa; it's very much a bamboo and rope-lashing affair—or it was then.'

Dominique smiled. 'And what about Kota Baharu?'

'Ah, well, it's very Malay—less Indian and Chinese influence; they fly kites and spin great tops. It's very interesting—they have a beach there called Pantai Cinta Berahi—the Beach of Passionate Love.'

Dominique sat back and Rory Jones could be seen to castigate himself humourlessly.

'Why did I bring that up?' he said wryly. 'You visibly shut the door in my face, speaking figuratively. Tell you what; for the rest of the meal I won't even mention love—passionate or otherwise.'

Dominique looked at him through her lashes but said nothing, and was saved by the arrival of their first course.

'On the other hand,' he said when they'd finished the course, 'we need to talk about something.'

'Could it be that this lack of anything to talk about is symptomatic of a lack of anything in common?' she suggested.

'No,' he disagreed. 'We've barely had time to establish that, except physically—and there are no problems there. No, I think it's to do with the fact that you're petrified of letting me come any closer to you. For reasons best known to yourself, but I'm beginning to get a pretty good idea of them. Never mind; I'll just soldier on. Now this is a very pleasant Pinot Noir; it should go well with your steak.'

Dominique couldn't fault the Pinot Noir but she drank it very sparingly; nor could she criticise the meal, but she refused dessert.

'Well, then, should we take a walk along the beach and come back for coffee and a liqueur?' he suggested.

'No, thank you. Why don't *you* tell me something about yourself while we have coffee here?' Dominique murmured.

He studied her for a moment. 'What would you like to know?' He ordered coffee but no liqueurs.

Dominique was silent and thoughtful until the coffee arrived, and he waited patiently, signing the bill at the same time. 'Do you have a career? Other than as a corporate businessman and grazier?' she asked at last.

'Yes—I'm a landscape gardener.'

Dominique choked on a sip of coffee.

Rory Jones smiled fleetingly. 'You didn't expect that. I wonder why?'

'I had this—playboy image of you, I guess. Hunting, fishing, shooting, skiing.'

'Who gave you that?'

Dominique looked away.

'I mean,' he persisted, 'you seemed so sure you knew nothing about me, apart from my complicated personal income-tax situation,' he said amusedly, and waited. But when she said nothing his eyes narrowed. 'Don't tell me you got in touch with our friend, Gayle?'

'She got in touch with me—in the first place,' Dominique said stiffly, then made a curious gesture of frustration. 'Yes, all right; I rang her last night.'

'Something I nobly refrained from doing,' he said.

'But, look, this gives me hope! I mean, that you should
be curious enough—'

'Curious enough to know what kind of person I was
being blackmailed by?' Dominique asked sardonically.

'Well—' he grimaced '—whatever. And she told you
I was a playboy?'

'Not—exactly, but close enough.'

'I thought Gayle was a friend!' he murmured with
mock sorrow.

'Oh, she is.' For a moment a glint of humour lit Dominique's eyes. 'In fact she's quite an admirer of yours.
But what she and *I* admire are not necessarily the same
thing.'

'In men?'

'In men, in wedding dresses...' Dominique bit her
lip. Why did I say that? she asked herself. An awful
Freudian slip? 'I didn't altogether like the wedding
dress she designed for your sister.'

'Neither did I,' he murmured, with a smile twisting
his lips. 'Does that mean I'm an arch-conservative on
the subject of wedding dresses? White and veils and so
on?' He gazed at her.

'I don't know; are you?' Dominique responded.

'Well, well—another tinge of curiosity?'

'Blame the Pinot Noir,' Dominique said prosaically.

'A glass and a half? Surely not,' he objected. 'What
else did Gayle contrive to misinform you about?'

'I don't know. Other than leaving out the landscape
gardener bit, not a lot, probably,' she said thoughtfully.
'Well, one other thing she said was that if you set your
mind to having—' She stopped warily.

'Having you?' he hazarded.

'Something like that. You were likely to get your

way. I don't know if you could call that misinformation, but it's something I take issue with all the same.'

'So I give you fair warning, Mr Jones?' he mocked, and added softly, 'We'll see.'

'I'm sure we will,' Dominique said graciously, and pushed her coffee-cup away. 'In the meantime, thank you for a delicious dinner—' She stopped abruptly as something behind him caught her eye.

'You're not going to stand up and walk out on me— just like that?' he said reproachfully. 'I am still a client, Miss Lindwall.'

Dominique made a lightning decision. 'All right; if you really want to walk on the beach.' She rose and said as naturally as she was able, 'Do we go this way? Through the gardens?' She gestured away from the main entrance to the restaurant.

'We...can.' He stood up himself and studied her narrowly for a moment. 'Do I have a time limit?'

'*Yes*. I mean...' Dominique took a tense little breath and his blue gaze raked her face.

Then he stepped round the table and took her arm and said quite pleasantly, 'We will go through the gardens.'

CHAPTER THREE

BUT when they came to the beach he took her hand, steered her to a bench and said quietly, 'I'm sure we don't need to do this as a forced march. Let's take a minute or two to regroup. Did I say something that seriously offended you?'

'No.' Dominique felt some of the tension within her seep away and discovered that what he'd said amused her. 'No. Not then,' she murmured wryly, and cast him a humorous sidelong look.

He raised his eyebrows quizzically. 'Something you found funny, then?'

'I...well, you said that as if you'd never, ever *dreamt* of offending me, which is what I found amusing, that's all. Are we going to walk—or talk? I'd rather walk if you don't mind.'

And she thought as he looked down at her that he had been going to say one thing then changed his mind and said another. He said, 'Really walk?'

She grimaced. 'Is there any other way?'

'I mean, shoes off and a good brisk pace?'

Dominique eyed the beach. The tide was low and lapping the sand gently. There was moonlight and a lot of stars in a dark, clear sky. 'All right.'

So he suggested that their shoes would be quite safe stowed out of sight beneath the bench, suggested that they should roll their trousers up a bit so that they wouldn't have to worry about getting them wet and told her that he would carry her bag.

'I can—'

But he took the small bronze bag with its long strap and slung it over his shoulder, then took her hand and said, 'Let's go.'

'Are you sure this isn't going to be a march?' she quipped.

He chuckled. 'You'll feel wonderful afterwards.'

Which was how she came to stride along at his side on the firm, damp sand, getting her feet wet at times but not unappreciative of the restorative powers of pleasant exercise after a meal and a shock, on a lovely starry night, with a companion who uncharacteristically said little—even a companion such as Rory Jones, whom she shouldn't be doing it with, but all the same...

'There,' he murmured when they got back to the bench half an hour later. 'Feel better?'

Dominique sank down slowly. 'Yes. Thank you,' she replied formally. 'I mean—' She stopped uncertainly.

'Like to tell me what happened now?' He sat down beside her.

'No...nothing; that is...no.'

'Dominique,' he chided, 'I know something did, so if you don't tell me I'm liable to imagine all sorts of things.'

'Yes, well, you do have a problem with your imagination, don't you?' she retorted, regaining her composure.

'Not concerning you,' he said with a mocking little smile lurking in his eyes. 'I have the most vivid memories of how your body feels beneath my hands, how it curves ripely then is slender, how your skin is like silk and velvet to touch, glossy in some places, more matt in others—memories of how your lips crushed—'

'Don't go on,' she said flatly.

'I thought you might like to contribute some of your memories—concerning me?' he suggested blandly.

'And I might have known this was all too good to be true.' She waved a hand to take in the moonlit beach and their walk and reached for her shoes, only to eye her sandy feet with frustration.

'Come upstairs to my room and we can wash and dry them properly, Dominique. I like your feet too, incidentally; they're very patrician—narrow and high—'

'You must think I'm either mad or as naïve as a schoolgirl!'

'Well, I can't help wondering if you lack poetry in your soul, which seems a pity. I mean, to look as you do, to be so exquisitely constructed, to respond physically so...*warmly* to a man yet—'

'Rory,' Dominique said wearily, 'would it be too much to ask you to give me a break? And, while I'm on the subject, would there be a tap beside the pool, say? And would you have a large, manly hanky that I could then dry my patrician feet on so I could go home in some comfort—you could always keep it and cherish it.'

There was a moment's silence, then he said rather drily, 'Not a naïve schoolgirl, no.'

'Now I've hurt your feelings; I'm sorry,' she said with a fleeting smile, but it faded almost immediately as she saw how he was looking at her. Not in a hurt or reproachful way at all, but with a considering, slightly contemptuous, tiger-like little glint in his eyes, in fact, that made her catch her breath involuntarily.

She thought of his earlier words about the jungle of love, and felt a little bit as if she was being stalked by a tiger—a big, beautiful and infinitely dangerous tiger...

But moments later she said exasperatedly, 'Look, I'm

a lost cause, Rory Jones! Why don't you just accept it? Even worse, I probably do lack poetry in my soul—your kind of flights of fancy anyway. I am an accountant after all—one of those dull, thorough kind of people. Doesn't that tell you a lot?'

He considered, but still with that steady, tiger-like little flame in his eyes. 'You're a mass of contradictions. I mean, what you do and what you say certainly contradict each other.'

'I know, I know,' she said with some irony. 'You've lost no opportunity to bring that home to me—I can only apologise. Will you give me my bag so I can go home?'

'All right, not a problem.' He handed her her bag gravely. 'And there is a tap near the pool; there are even towels available to guests. Shall we go and wash our feet?' He stood up.

'And then?' She looked up at him uncertainly.

'You can go home.'

Just like that, she thought as she drove home. A courteous yet curiously indifferent parting. So why do I feel—all tense, and as if I haven't heard the end of this? And how did he somehow or other contrive to make me feel as if I'd significantly lowered myself in his estimation—why on earth am I even thinking about it in this way?

But as she lay in bed later she was still thinking about it, remembering the pleasantness of their walk along the beach—thinking, in fact, more of that than of the shock of looking across the restaurant and seeing Bryce Denver, to whom she'd been engaged to marry not that long ago, waiting to be guided to a table with a striking blonde at his side...

* * *

By the next morning, however, she'd recovered her sense of balance, as she termed it to herself—her perception of Rory Jones as an arch-opportunist who was the most unlikely landscape gardener and much *more* likely to be a very seasoned, dangerous playboy, in other words. And on the subject of her former fiancé she had resolutely and coldly closed her mind.

Her sense of balance was brutally toppled at work a few hours later.

'Dominique, Mr Conrod is coming to see you,' Sally informed her. 'In about ten minutes.'

'What about?' Dominique sighed irritably.

'His secretary didn't see fit to tell me that so I didn't enquire,' Sally replied virtuously. 'I'll just tidy you up a bit.'

'Sally!' Dominique looked even more irritated as Sally started to pile papers in neat heaps.

'We might as well make a good impression—it's not often he goes to see people rather than having them come to him. Why, it's almost like the mountain coming to Mohammed. Why don't you put your jacket on and run a comb through your hair?'

But Dominique was not given a chance to do either of these things as Frank Conrod entered her office with a breezy triple knock. 'Ah, there you are, Dominique—how are you, my dear? Looking as attractive as ever, I see,' he said in an avuncular manner as he lowered his portly frame into a chair. 'Got some good news for you!'

Dominique blinked and murmured a greeting as she thought dazedly, Not a partnership...could it be?

But three minutes later she was staring in disbelief

and outrage at Frank Conrod. 'You mean he wants *me* to do a personal audit for him?'

'That's exactly it. He reckons it should only take you a week and he will give you a guided tour of all his—affairs. He does have a pretty complicated—'

'Personal income-tax situation,' Dominique said through her teeth. 'I don't believe it!'

Frank Conrod frowned. 'Dominique, the Jones family is one of our largest clients; we are the external auditors for all their companies and Rory Jones is effectively head of the clan since the recent death of his father.'

'But look, I'm snowed under, Mr Conrod,' she protested. 'Nor do I need a personally guided tour of his affairs; all I need is the paperwork. Or, conversely, all he needs—if he's genuine about this—is a clerk—'

'Dominique, it's because of the recent death of his father that his affairs have become much more complicated. Believe me, he needs some expert assessment and advice.

'If I had not believed you were capable of coping with this, I would not have assigned Rory Jones to you after Lancelot rather unexpectedly and unfortunately retired. But not only did you pass out second in the state in your accountancy final, you've *proved* yourself here; in fact you show brilliance and flair, your grasp of tax law is pretty nearly phenomenal for one so young, you've coped extremely well with a heavy workload over the last months and this is, is it not, the kind of progressive firm where flair and brilliance are rewarded, irrespective of sex and age?'

'I...yes! I mean...' She paused, then went on in less annoyed tones, 'I appreciate that, Mr Conrod.' Then she stopped and stared at him.

'And I will be appointing a junior accountant to assist

you here while you're away. He can get through all the
leg-work you're so snowed under with at the moment—
I had had that in mind anyway.' Frank Conrod rose and
smiled down at her warmly. 'I know you won't let me
down, Dominique.'

'The *bastard*...'

'Mr Conrod?' Sally asked, coming in moments after
the senior partner had left. 'Oh, I don't know about that!
He—'

'Not *him*,' Dominique said intensely. 'Although I
wouldn't be surprised if he's let himself be conned into
this because he's a man! I mean Mr Emory Jones.'

Sally blinked. 'Well, I have to tell you I rather liked
him, Dominique—'

'You would,' Dominique said witheringly, and sat
down disgustedly.

'What's that supposed to mean?' Sally enquired, un-
offended.

But instead of enlightening her Dominique told her
what had transpired with Mr Conrod.

'Now that sounds jolly—jolly!' Sally said enthusiastically. 'A week away from the mill with a rather
divine member of the opposite sex who is as wealthy
as—'

'How do you know he's divine?' Dominique said
with an exasperated frown.

'Well, you've only got to look at him—'

'Looks don't mean everything,' Dominique said scathingly.

'No, but they do help,' Sally countered. 'And I actually thought he was rather nice. Unless,' she added
slyly, 'you're off men? Particularly good-looking men?'

Dominique didn't bother to dissemble. 'I'm not going

to deny the charge, Sally; I'm sick to death of the lot of them if you must know!'

'You'll get over it,' Sally said kindly. 'I know it's not pleasant to have an engagement broken on you, but Bryce Denver was never the right one for you in the first place, and one day you'll see how lucky you were!'

'How do you—how do *you* know he wasn't the right one for me?'

'Because you were too clever for him, Dominique,' Sally said simply. 'Everyone in the firm knew that bar *him*. All the same, when an opportunity came up in commerce he didn't take much persuading to leave the firm and the profession, so perhaps he did see the contrast.

'But what he did want above all was a wife with her own means as well as a wife with undoubted brains— very ambitious was our Bryce,' Sally added, and then concluded, 'And if all of that's not bad enough, if the rumours are true he wasn't being faithful to you even while you were engaged.'

Dominique stared at her and discovered herself to be breathing heavily. It was in this little interim that the phone rang.

Sally picked it up and said moments later, covering the mouthpiece, 'It's for you. Mr Emory Jones.'

'Tell him I'm not here. Take a message.'

'I—'

'Do it, Sally,' Dominique said brusquely.

Sally returned the receiver to her ear. 'She must have just slipped out, Mr Jones! I'm sorry about that; can I take a message? Yes… Yes, she has. Yes… Yes… Fine, I've got that; I'll tell her. I'm sure she'll be ready and waiting, Mr Jones. Goodbye!'

'*What?*' Dominique demanded through her teeth.

'He'll pick you up here at noon tomorrow—a bit like *High Noon* if I'm not mistaken—er—sorry, Dominique,' Sally said unrepentantly. 'You'll be flying out to Mount Livingstone, one of his cattle stations, for a few days. You'll need light but practical clothing for daytime and something a bit warmer for evening. That's all.'

'*All?*'

That evening Dominique treated herself to a glass of white wine with the solitary dinner that she cooked for herself. She was very tired, having spent the afternoon going through urgent matters with the junior assigned to her—something that would also be occupying her the following morning—and she had yet to pack a bag for a sojourn on a cattle station.

When the phone rang she was tempted to ignore it in case it was Rory Jones, then was sorry that she hadn't stuck to this because it was worse, if anything—it was Bryce.

'Hello, Dominique,' he said quietly down the line. 'I saw you last night and I thought I'd just ring up and say hello.'

'For old times' sake?' Dominique said with irony, after a moment of speechlessness.

'Dom, you know the one thing I wanted to achieve for us was an...amicable parting of the ways,' he said reproachfully.

'I know,' she agreed. 'Perhaps because I was the one with a wedding dress hanging in my closet, it was a bit harder for me to achieve than you,' she suggested.

'But...' he hesitated '...you are getting over it, aren't you? I mean, the solution was in your hands; it's nine months now and…' another slight hesitation '…you *were* being wined and dined last night.'

'So I was.'

'Anything serious on the go? Who was he?'

Dominique sat down and stared at the miniature of her mother as an incredible intuition seized her. She had not heard from Bryce in nine months. So why now, and after he'd seen her with someone else?

'Rory Jones,' she said casually. 'I don't know if you've heard of the Jones family?'

There was an audible intake of breath. Then Bryce Denver said grimly, 'Yes, I have; I've met some of them, although not him—Dominique…take care.'

'Why? He's—a lot of fun actually.'

'He's had plenty of women.'

'Oh, that.'

'Dom, I wouldn't want to see you get hurt. I still…' a pause '…care a lot about you, you know.'

Or is it that you prefer to think of me pining away for you, Bryce? she thought, and was suddenly so furious that she could barely breathe. 'I won't,' she said gaily. 'Don't you worry about me, Bryce. And I thought the girl you were with was just lovely,' she managed to add, in a way that sounded genuine yet completely impersonal.

'We're not serious,' he said abruptly.

'Oh, what a pity! I thought she might have been the one you couldn't do without while you were engaged to me.'

He swore. '*Are* you serious about this Jones character?'

'Well, I think I might be, Bryce, but it's early days yet.' Dominique could not for the life of her resist saying lightly, 'I'm just going to play it by ear for a while.

I wouldn't want to make the same mistakes I made with you, would I? And he's rather hard to resist. But, anyway, it was really nice of you to give me a call—you're right; there's no reason for us not to let bygones be bygones.' And she put the phone down.

But she also said aloud to herself, 'I don't *believe* it! Am I *imagining* it?'

And as she lay in bed later she remembered Sally's words and discovered herself face to face again with the lowering knowledge that she'd been taken in by Bryce's looks and charm, that she'd been the *last* one to know that he was seeing someone else only weeks before the wedding. And then had to confront him with it... To be told that it was her own fault for some very specific reasons.

And now this—while *he* didn't want her, he didn't want anyone else to have her. Or was he thinking of having another go at securing his future with her money?

'Is it any wonder,' she asked herself aloud, 'that I don't like good-looking, charming men?'

Her disposition towards all men was not improved the next day, and even her disgust at Bryce didn't make her feel more cordial towards one Emory Jones. Indeed, on top of her outrage at being outmanoeuvred the way she had, she was disgusted with herself for stooping to using him—not on Bryce's account but her own.

He didn't fail to notice her outrage as he assisted her into the Land Rover and handed her her briefcase.

'Hello, Miss Lindwall. How are you? I'm fine, thank you, and yes, it is a lovely day,' he drawled as he swung himself into the driver's seat.

'Look, I'm here,' she said tightly. 'Don't expect me to make pleasant conversation on top of it.'

'You feel—hard done by?' he queried politely.

'*No.* I feel utterly contemptuous of a man who has to resort to these tactics!'

He laughed softly. 'Nevertheless you came, Dominique.'

'I was given no choice. Where is this Mount Livingstone, and how long do we have to fly to get to it?'

'Near Birdsville—'

'*Birdsville,*' Dominique repeated.

'It's not the end of the world, although it's not far from it,' he conceded.

'It's on the edge of the Simpson Desert! It's a thousand miles away!'

'Yes, it's quite an experience,' he agreed. 'If you'd taken my call yesterday, instead of hiding behind your secretary, I'd have been able to fill you in then. It might not have come as such a shock.'

'Oh, yes, it would! I mean—' She stopped and bit her lip.

'You haven't brought the right things to wear?' he said gravely.

She cast him a very speaking look.

'I'm abashed,' he said immediately. 'I quite thought all this was the injured outpouring of an ultra-sophisticated girl who can't live without hairdressers, manicures and six changes of clothes a day.'

'I go to the hairdresser once a month, my hair curls naturally and I manicure my own nails,' Dominique said frostily. 'I never change my clothes six times a day and I work extremely hard for a—well, I do work very hard.'

'Then what is it?'

'As if you don't very well know!'

'What I was trying to say is that if you're a city born and bred kind of girl, with a horror or fear of the out-back—'

'I'm *not*. Well, I haven't had a lot of experience of it—'

'Then you're in for a pleasant surprise, Dominique,' he said as he steered the Land Rover expertly down the Pacific Highway towards Coolangatta Airport. 'The contrast, the sense of wilderness is a very agreeable ex-perience—did I get you wrong, by the way?'

'What do you *mean*?'

'Well, as one who is off to explore the unbeaten tracks of Sarawak shortly, I thought—'

'I say it again—you know very well why I'm ob-jecting to this, Emory Jones,' Dominique interrupted ac-idly and wearily. 'Don't think any of this—trying to tie me up in knots deceives me for a moment.'

'Yes, I do—know very well,' he said promptly. 'You're afraid of being stuck out on a cattle station near Birdsville with me because there will be nowhere to run to if you once again succumb to my embraces despite all your strength of will and better judgement.'

'You're— That's diabolical,' Dominique said on an indrawn breath. 'Nor do I understand! Only two nights ago you looked at me as if...as if I was *beneath* you.'

He raised a quizzical eyebrow. 'I discovered that was a temporary state of affairs. Sorry.'

Dominique swore not quite beneath her breath.

His lips quirked. 'Don't mind me,' he said softly, and added, 'We're here.'

'That's another thing,' Dominique said. 'I'm not a fan of flying around the place in little planes!'

'Ah, but I'm a very good pilot—you'll be quite safe with me.'

'It would help if you relaxed a bit,' he drawled, after they'd taken off in the Piper Cherokee. 'I'm about to show you some wondrous sights.'

'Such as?' Dominique enquired coldly as the plane gained height. She was sitting beside him, her hands clasped whitely in her lap, watching what his hands did instead of looking at the ground that seemed to be receding so agonisingly slowly beneath them.

He had headphones on and was wearing a khaki bomber jacket, plain white shirt, brown moleskins and hiking boots—and she realised with a sudden pang that it was getting harder not to be affected by his sheer masculinity and how incredibly competent he looked as he checked switches and held the half-wheel, and how well modulated his voice was as he spoke to the Coolangatta tower through the mike attached to his headphones, how beautiful his hands were...

'You've heard of Cyclone Sadie, I presume?'

'Yes,' she said uncertainly. 'Didn't it menace Cairns and the far north a few weeks ago?'

'Sure did. Then it moved inland and weakened to a rain depression and dumped over six inches over most of the central west of the state, thus generating a great flood that's bringing new life and hope to the parched south-west. It's quite a sight.'

'A flood?'

'Well, in this kind of country it's a different kind of flood; the water spreads and spreads slowly and runs in shallow channels; that's why they call it "channel country". And it's a magnificent sight from the air—well, it will be from the upper reaches of Cooper Creek; a web of thousands of fingers of water spreading across the land.'

'So,' Dominique said, interested in spite of herself, 'is it raining there?'

'No. That's the miracle of it. Mount Livingstone and around Windorah and Birdsville haven't had a drop—it's eight-inches-a-year territory out there—but this water seeps through and nourishes the earth so that there'll be grazing again, and it's certainly needed. The last big wet we had was in 1990.'

'Tell me about Mount Livingstone,' Dominique said slowly.

'It covers about ten thousand square kilometres and in good seasons we can carry about thirty thousand head of cattle. At the moment we're only running to half-capacity.'

'I've heard of Cooper Creek; who hasn't?' she said involuntarily. 'Doesn't it eventually run into Lake Eyre?'

'Yes, but this water will take months to get there. Feeling better?'

'Yes. Thank you. Are you close to Sturt's Stony Desert? I've heard of that too.'

'Uh-huh.' He banked slightly and changed course so that they were flying away from the coast.

'Were you born to this—I mean, out there?'

'No, I was born in Brisbane, but Mount Livingstone has been in the family for a long time.'

'I would have thought…you'd be anything but a landscape gardener,' she mused.

He grinned. 'I'm a botanist, actually.'

'Why did you say…?'

'Well, I enjoy landscaping gardens; it's sort of a spin-off from being a botanist, anyway.'

'Like Sir Joseph Banks,' she said unthinkingly.

'I didn't know he was a landscape gardener.' He looked at her amusedly.

'Neither did I. I was thinking more along the lines of—well, he was supposed to be a bit of a lad too, wasn't he?'

'Too—was he?'

'Going by the television programme I saw on the subject, he was,' she said a bit drily. 'Definitely not as dour and decorous as Captain Cook. He even tried to smuggle a girl dressed as a sailor aboard the *Endeavour* apparently.'

'How decadent,' Rory Jones murmured. 'I've never had to go to those lengths.'

'I believe you,' Dominique said tartly. 'And now you've inherited it all. According to Mr Conrod.'

'More or less. Which is why I need you, dear Dominique,' he said, and studied her with a pair of guileless blue eyes. 'We've been left with an extremely complicated set of family companies, trusts et cetera, and I felt it could only help you to see them at first hand.'

Dominique sat back and sighed.

'You don't feel up to it?' he queried after a moment.

'I'm sure I will be,' she said slowly.

'You just have to get into the right frame of mind?' he suggested.

'Perhaps. I was only wondering how difficult you're going to make it, Mr…Rory.'

'We'll see,' was all he said, and turned his attention to pointing out landmarks along their flight path.

And, indeed, the confluence of the Thomson River and the Barcoo, creating Cooper Creek, was a spectacular sight from the air.

'Unbelievable!' Dominique murmured once. 'But what about stock, and all the roads that have been cut?'

'They've had plenty of warning, time to get in provisions and move stock to high ground, and there are not many people moving around this part of the outback at the moment; it's too hot, for one thing—forty degrees Celsius.'

Dominique grimaced.

'What I'd really like to do is bring you back later in the year; the wild flowers will transform the desert in about September, after this flood. There'll be kangaroos everywhere and emus trailing families of striped chicks—all sorts of bird life; it's quite a sight.'

'Thank you for *this*,' Dominique said impulsively, and added as he raised a wry eyebrow at her, 'Which is not to say I will immediately be made over into...' She paused and searched for words.

'All sweetness and light?' Rory said pensively.

'No, I won't,' she answered lightly but definitely. 'This *has* been an incredible experience, though.' She looked down as they floated through the blue sky, at the shining sheets of water spread out over the ochre-brown earth below. 'I feel as if I've seen the true heart of Australia—well, we can't be that far from it, can we?'

'As those kinds of distances go, no. We're pretty close to the South Australian and Northern Territory borders. We're not far from where John Flynn set up the Inland Mission and the Royal Flying Doctor Service, or from where Burke and Wills perished near Innamincka. They say, as a matter of interest, if you can find your way by air to Birdsville, you could find your way to anywhere on earth.'

Dominique stiffened slightly. 'What do you mean?'

'Well, apart from a few low-watt radio beacons it's seat-of-the-pants flying—compass and watch kind of thing.'

'Do you mean to tell me...?' She stared at him open-mouthed.

'No, I don't; I'm only having you on. I have a couple of pretty sophisticated instruments on board to tell me where I am.' He laughed at her. 'A lot of people do know this country like the back of their hand, though.'

Dominique looked out again at the endless, feature-less plain of water, red earth and scrub, and blinked a couple of times. 'I don't know why but it's—rather ro-mantic, isn't it? I don't mean—'

'Perish the thought! No,' he relented. 'I know what you mean. The red heart of Australia has that effect on a lot of people. Well, you only have one more challenge to face today, Dominique.'

'What's that?'

'There's Mount Livingstone ahead of us; my sister is in residence—the one whose wedding dress you didn't like—and—' he stopped and swore '—a few other peo-ple by the look of it.'

Dominique looked down and saw three light planes on the dusty runway beside a sprawl of green-roofed buildings.

'Dominique, this is my sister, Belinda Miller—Belinda, this is Dominique Lindwall, my accountant.'

'Goodness gracious me, Rory!' Belinda Miller, who was as dark as her brother was fair, was also svelte, bright-eyed and one of those people who obviously spoke their mind. 'I've heard of all sorts of names for it before, but never accountant! Dominique. *Lindwall*,' she mused with a frown.

'See what I mean?' Rory murmured to Dominique, and turned back to his sister. 'Dear heart, how many times do I have to tell you that you have an awful propensity for putting your foot in your mouth? But what the hell is going on?'

'Nothing's going on that shouldn't be going on, Rory, dear,' Belinda Miller retorted. 'I'm having a party, that's all. And if you'd thought to give me some notice instead of arriving out of the blue I'd have been able to tell you about it. Not that it matters; now you're here, you're very welcome. There's just one problem. I have no free guest rooms left—or is it such a problem?' And she eyed her brother narrowly.

'What do you mean?' he shot back dangerously.

'Well, there's your room,' she replied ingenuously.

Rory Jones said something pithy and uncomplimentary, but Belinda appeared totally unfloored and turned her attention back to Dominique, with a frown in her dark eyes. 'But, let me see, don't I know you?' she murmured after a tense moment.

'No,' Dominique said coolly.

'Then I know *of* you—that's it!' She snapped her fingers. 'Aren't you the girl Bryce Denver left virtually at the altar?'

CHAPTER FOUR

'DOMINIQUE—'

'No, it's no good,' Dominique said curtly. 'I want to be off this place first thing in the morning. And when I get back to the office I'll tell Mr Conrod that I don't wish to handle you any longer *even* if it costs me my job.'

Rory Jones closed the door and advanced into the middle of his bedroom. It was a big, old-fashioned but comfortable room, with a huge four-poster bed without hangings, two winged armchairs in front of a fireplace, a mahogany dresser and wardrobe, chintzy curtains and a half-glass door that led out onto a veranda.

The whole homestead, from the little Dominique had seen of it, seemed old-fashioned but huge, sprawling and comfortable, with massive pieces of well-polished furniture, leaded lights over doors—and the hum of a powerful generator in the background.

'Dominique, I apologise for my sister,' he said evenly.

'That's as may be; it's still not going to work,' Dominique said intensely. '*Everyone* is going to…raise their eyebrows at your accountant—'

'It's not my fault you're the best-looking, not to say most unlikely-looking accountant in the country,' he pointed out drily.

'It is your fault, however, that you have such a play-boy image that no woman in your company can be

57

thought of as anything else but your—girlfriend, for want of a more accurate term,' she said crisply.

'Look, is that the real problem? I mean, I feel sure you're perfectly capable of disabusing people of that notion—you didn't think twice about telling Belinda that you would no more dream of consorting with me than a snake. And, no, hang on—' he waved a negligent hand but his eyes glinted '—you can rest assured your "momentary aberration" with me will be our secret.'

'I hate you,' Dominique said very quietly, and sat down unexpectedly on the bed. 'And no, that's only *one* of the problems. Did you honestly imagine I'd be delighted to be introduced to everyone as the girl Bryce Denver left at the altar?'

'Dominique—'

But she went on angrily, 'And if you think I'd consent to sharing a bedroom with you you must be out of your mind, Rory Jones!'

'You won't have to share it with me; I'll find somewhere else.'

'I still don't want to stay here,' she said, with a toss of her head as she looked around with bitter tears not far away.

'Because it would make you *think* of us sharing it?' he suggested coolly.

For a moment, as she glared up at him, her expression defied description.

'OK, OK, I'm sorry,' he said wryly, but sobered suddenly and sat down beside her. 'What Belinda said was unforgivable, and I assume it has to be true for you to react this way.'

Dominique looked away and hoped that the tears pricking her eyelids didn't get out of hand.

'But,' he went on, 'it's no reason to jeopardise your

job. Was it this Bryce Denver you saw at the Mirage the other night, by any chance?'

Surprise caused Dominique to turn her head towards him. 'How...?' The words got caught in her throat.

He smiled, but unamusedly. 'I think I have extrasensory perception where you're concerned.'

She shrugged and looked down at her hands. 'Yes,' she said abruptly.

'So it still hurts a hell of a lot?'

'It...' She stopped and sniffed. 'It's not the easiest thing to live with, no.'

'Even though he must have been mad?'

'You don't... You don't know him and you don't really know me, Mr...Rory, so you're not qualified to comment.'

'Very well,' he replied equably. 'I do aim to get to know you better, but before you get all bitter and twisted about that—'

'I'm *not*,' she denied angrily.

'Could have fooled me,' he drawled.

Dominique tossed her head again; her eyes glinted green fire. 'Then I'll *show* you!'

'That's my girl.' He patted her hand and stood up. 'Belinda's not a bad kid, by the way. She's been dreadfully indulged all her life—that's the problem. But I'll make sure there are no more comments for you to take exception to. And, don't forget, I'm behind you all the way,' he said kindly, and added, 'Dinner will be ready in half an hour. I'll come and get you.' And he strolled out of the room.

Dominique stared after him, her eyes now registering the fact that she'd walked straight into the trap he'd set for her; then, as the door closed softly, she dropped her head into her hands and ground her teeth in frustration.

*   *   *

She discovered that there was a modern bathroom attached to the room so she showered and changed into
the one dress she'd brought—a black georgette patterned with little flax-coloured and green flowers and
styled in a simple, waistless style to mid-calf, with a
scooped neckline and short sleeves. It came with a flax-
coloured linen waistcoat, which she put on too.

After a fiery sunset, the scorching air had cooled considerably, and she tied back her hair, which was glinting
gold and curling madly after her shower, with a green
scarf. Black suede flatties completed the outfit and she
made up her face lightly and painted her lips a subtle
bronze-pink. As a final touch, and with a touch of de-
fiance, she sprayed some Poison from its black and
green flask onto her neck.

As she waited for Rory she paced around the room
and noted that there were some lovely things in it—a
beautiful porcelain ewer and basin patterned with
lovely, blowsy yellow roses, two Georgian solid silver
candlesticks on the dresser, hand-crocheted trims to the
linen pillowcases…

There was a knock on the door and it swung open to
reveal Rory. 'Ah, you're ready,' he murmured, and said
nothing more as their gazes locked in a curiously tense
little moment.

A moment, Dominique thought, when she couldn't
deny, much as she would have loved to, that she was
as suddenly aware of him as he was of her. A moment
when they seemed to take each other in from head to
toe—when it was impossible for her to resist the impact
of Rory Jones, big and almost take-your-breath-away
good-looking in navy blue trousers and a blue and white
striped shirt with a white open collar.

But it wasn't only that. It wasn't the shocking little

memory of his hands on her hips, his mouth on hers, the way they'd breathed as one, moved as one, the hard strength of his body against hers...

'What?' he said softly.

'Nothing. Nothing,' she replied hastily, and swallowed. 'Well, you'd better lead on.'

He smiled—a fleeting movement of his lips—but said gravely, 'I would offer to hold your hand as I lead you into this den of the unknown, but that could compromise your position as my accountant—the guests are all assembled.'

Dominique clicked her teeth in exasperation. 'How *many*?'

'About ten, although I haven't done a headcount. You might even like them.'

'Don't count on it,' she said tartly, and moved purposefully towards the door. He stood aside.

'Don't tell me—Gayle Gyngell!' Belinda Miller said as she scanned Dominique with her head to one side. She herself was wearing sulphur-yellow—culottes and a silk blouse.

'No. Lizzie Collins,' Dominique replied coolly.

Belinda smiled, a bit like a cat. 'Rather nice, anyway. Come and meet everyone. This is my husband, Luke, and...' She did the rounds of the ten or so people in the room, finishing, 'Got that, or did I go too fast?'

'Not at all. How do you do?' Dominique said at large, and smiled slightly.

'And this, folks, is Dominique Lindwall—Rory's accountant.' She paused, opened her mouth to say more, but Rory Jones intervened.

'Can I get you a drink, Dominique?'

Dominique glanced around. 'A dry sherry, thank you.'

He moved away and Belinda sat down and, surprisingly, patted the settee beside her. When Dominique sat down after a slight pause, she said, 'Don't mind me too much. I'm told I was terribly indulged as a child, and a lot of people tell me they don't know how Luke copes—don't they, darling?' she added, with a throwaway smile towards her husband, and continued, barely taking a breath, 'What interests me, though, is how any woman is going to cope with Rory—not that he was terribly indulged, the opposite if anything, but—'

'Bel, take a breath and let Dominique do the same,' Rory admonished her from above them, and handed Dominique a glass of sherry. 'She's had a rather rough initiation to the Jones clan, I'm afraid,' he added, with an oddly significant look at Dominique.

'Oh.' His sister gazed at Dominique frankly and said, 'Do you frighten easily, then?'

'No—do I look as if I do?' Dominique asked with a grimace.

'Well, you did look a little shell-shocked earlier.' Belinda shrugged. 'My fault, probably, but anyway, tell me about yourself; are you really an accountant?'

Dominique cast a fleeting, sorely tired look upwards at Rory, but when he started to answer for her interrupted to say, 'Yes, I am—I know it seems to be an odd occupation for a girl, but I followed in my father's footsteps. And the partner in the firm I work for, who handled your family affairs, retired rather suddenly recently because of ill-health, so that's how I come to be—'

'Ah, Lancelot!' Belinda said with a grin. 'He didn't

really approve of me—I wonder if you're going to be the same, Dominique? In the meantime, dinner's ready.'

The table was large, old and oak, the crystal glinted, the china was beautiful and the meal delicious. At times Dominique found it hard to believe that she was dining not far, as those distances went, from the Birdsville Track. The conversation was wide-ranging and stimulating, although it did have a tendency to keep coming back to the approaching flood waters.

But the guests at Belinda's party turned out to be friendly people, mostly from the district, who would all be flying home in the morning. And Luke Miller turned out to be big and quiet, the complete opposite of his aggressive, outspoken wife.

Dominique learnt that he'd been born in the area, of another old grazing family. She also learnt that Belinda Miller's present project was the restoration of the Mount Livingstone homestead to its 'former glory', as she termed it, and that Belinda needed frequent breaks from this lifestyle, however, whereas Luke was quite happy to stay put for ever—he now managed Mount Livingstone. She took a few moments to muse upon the attraction of opposites.

The last person she could imagine Luke Miller marrying, particularly when she was clothed in a silver strapless wedding dress, was Rory Jones's articulate sister, who also had that unmistakable air of having been born with a silver spoon in her mouth.

She was still thinking about this after dinner, when Rory found her alone on the veranda, and was also wondering if she could escape the party unnoticed. She stared out over the dark landscape through an eerie sort of mist. 'Penny for them?' he said.

She jumped a little.

'Did I frighten you? Sorry.'

'No, you didn't frighten me—I'm not as easily frightened as you all seem to think,' she replied. 'What is that mist?'

'It's the lake where we cool our water. Do you know anything about the great artesian basin? I'll tell you anyway,' he said obligingly.

'So,' Dominique said a few minutes later, 'it actually comes up out of the ground through these bores, hot— that's very handy!'

'If this wasn't a part of the world where cold water is preferable for the most part,' he said with a grin. 'It's not fit for human consumption, although we use it for everything else and stock can survive on it; you can use it for irrigation, and it's what's made this whole area viable.'

'I see.'

'Yes, interesting, isn't it?'

'It is.'

'And dinner wasn't so bad, was it?'

She turned to look at him at last. 'No.'

'Does that mean you'll stay?'

Their gazes locked and held, and it struck Dominique that for all his sister's outspokenness there was no doubt that Rory Jones was very much the boss on Mount Livingstone. 'How come,' she said involuntarily, 'your sister was spoiled rotten but not you? According to her, anyway.'

'Ah, that goes back to our parents. Should we sit down out here and discuss this phenomenon in depth?' he asked. 'Or would you like to go back inside for your coffee? I've been deputised to tell you it's being served in the lounge, but I could always bring ours out here. I should imagine the festivities will really begin after coffee.'

Dominique hesitated and bit her lip.

'Caught between the devil and the deep blue sea,' Rory Jones murmured, his blue eyes alight with devilish amusement, and waited. But the matter was settled unexpectedly. Belinda appeared on the veranda, wheeling a small trolley.

'There you are,' she said genially, but went on with a wicked little glint in her dark eyes, 'I've given everyone else their coffee so I'll leave the trolley with you. I told the others you'd most likely be discussing business out here; it's a *wonderfully* fine night for it! Don't you agree?'

'Thank you, Bel,' Rory Jones said, but with more than a hint of steel in his voice.

To which his sister took exception in the form of tossing her head, but she retreated inside speechless nevertheless.

Dominique also said nothing, but her expression said it for her.

He raised a wry eyebrow at her as he poured the coffee from a silver pot. 'You'll learn soon enough that you just have to be firm with Belinda. Do sit down.' He gestured to the wooden bench that ran along the wall, handed her a cup of black coffee with one sugar, which was exactly how she liked it, as he must have observed, and leant back against the veranda railing with his own. 'Where were we?'

Dominique sat down and glanced at him through her lashes. 'As if you didn't know.'

'You're right—why was Belinda spoilt and I wasn't? Our parents were rather mismatched, unfortunately. They certainly spent nearly all their married life warring with each other, and, I'm afraid, as kids we got split into camps. My mother fought her brand of warfare through us, or tried to, which is to say that although my father made it clear he wouldn't allow her to spoil me rotten, when Belinda came along five years later—the mind boggles when one tries to imagine how *that* happened—because she was a girl, she won with her.'

'That's—' Dominique frowned '—incredible. How could two adults…?'

'Ah, it's amazing what two adults who are locked into a love-hate relationship can do.'

'But—' Dominique shook her head as if to clear it '—you don't even sound particularly bitter about it. It's amazing you and your sister don't hate each other.'

'I've always thought I was a particularly well-adjusted person, as a matter of fact. I'm rather fond of Belinda, who is—' he smiled unexpectedly '—curiously protective of me, despite her faults. And they're not so great, actually; I think she just bears those outspoken genes, and there's not a lot one can do about one's genes, is there?'

'I suppose not,' Dominique said slowly. 'After all, you're pretty…well, you don't exactly hide your own light under a bushel.'

He laughed but said with an oddly searching look, 'Unlike you, Dominique. Did you get that from your father, as well as your passion for accountability?'

'No, my mother,' Dominique said without thinking, then bit her lip. 'I mean, what makes you think I'm…well, an introvert as opposed to being an extrovert?'

He paused and narrowed his eyes, then said quietly, 'Put it this way; I can't imagine Belinda being left at the altar.'

Dominique moved abruptly and spilt some coffee into her saucer.

'Here, let me,' he said immediately, and took both cup and saucer from her, blotted the saucer with a damask napkin, and handed them back to her.

'Thank you—you are as bad as your sister,' she said tautly.

'No, I'm not,' he commented. 'I'm merely a man who has kissed you and handled you fairly intimately, and is now trying to get to know you better—I know things should be done the other way round, but it didn't work out that way for us, Dominique, did it? You've always shown a preference for dancing, embracing, even walking with me rather than talking. So you can't altogether blame me for trying to—work my way towards some kind of light.'

'You also never give up, do you?' Dominique whispered.

'No.' He said it briefly and definitely, and as she looked across at him she saw that considering, tiger-like look in his eyes again and realised that there was much more to Rory Jones than the playboy personality she liked to ascribe to him. Something tougher and deeper. And she shivered inwardly for some reason.

Then his look changed and he said lightly, 'Have we reached another impasse?'

'Probably,' she said huskily, and with nothing like the definition she'd have liked to employ. But the truth of the matter was that she felt curiously jumpy and as if her nerves were exposed—and all because of him, damn him, she thought.

'Then why don't we join the rest of them? Unless you're preparing to scuttle off to bed—my bed,' he said consideringly. 'Which could be a cold, lonely place without me.'

'I've no intention of scuttling off to your bed yet, but when I do I'll be most surprised if I don't sleep like a log,' she said proudly, damning her jumpy nerves as well.

He looked at her expressionlessly for a long moment, then smiled at her with real amusement. 'So be it,' he murmured, straightening up.

But Dominique said, 'Just a minute, Mr Jones. I know why you're laughing at me. I know you feel you've conned me at least twice tonight into doing things I didn't particularly want to do—'

'Well, that you've avowed not to do, anyway,' he drawled. 'Either to me or yourself—but do go on.' He waited politely.

'Just this—it's a far cry from conning me into your bed. Nor does it cause you to rise in my estimation in the slightest.'

'It's funny you should say that—in the light of how we stand in each *other's* estimations in certain respects. After you, Miss Lindwall.'

So Dominique parted and inwardly simmered for the next couple of hours. And when the lights were dimmed, the rugs rolled up, music put on, she thought wearily, I don't know why I should have expected anything good to come out of this day, but surely someone could have spared me this...?

Of course no one did, and so she danced a couple of times, and at other times took care to stay as far away as possible from Rory Jones. Nor did he make any move towards her until he'd danced with every woman in the room and he and Belinda had done the twist to everyone's enthusiastic applause.

It was during the applause that she looked around and decided that she definitely would slip away this time, only to find him right behind her as the music changed and someone dimmed the lights even further.

'Oh, no...' she whispered as he took her hand.

'Then you shouldn't have stayed,' he said barely audibly, and touched his fingertips to her suddenly hot cheek. 'Isn't that like asking for trouble?'

'Please—no,' she said raggedly.

'And is this not our kind of music, Dominique?' he went on, ignoring her words and taking her in his arms. 'I seem to remember that it is.'

She looked up into his eyes agitatedly, saw the mockery and the hint of steel in them, and knew suddenly that she was going to pay in some form tonight for allowing Rory Jones all the liberties she had, then walking away from him as she had... And pay in kind, possibly.

'Don't look like that,' he murmured drily. 'It's no tragedy. Why don't you just dance, Dominique? As we know you can. Or do you really want everyone to start wondering what exactly does go on between me and my accountant?'

She closed her eyes briefly, then started to move to the music, but it brought her no relief as he said, 'Well, that makes it three times in the space of a few short hours now, Miss Lindwall.'

She knew exactly what he meant and didn't even try to refute the charge.

But he went even further as they moved together to the slow music amidst the other couples, but for her alone to hear. 'Why don't you tell me you hate me,

Dominique? I quite miss it when you don't—have you ever stopped to contemplate that *you* could be indulging in a love-hate relationship with a man, by the way? I know the thought of it shocked you earlier, but it seems to me that it bears thinking about—'

But she could stand no more, whatever the consequences, and she pulled herself out of his arms and slipped blindly through the other dancers.

Unfortunately, she took a wrong turning, which saw her arrive at his bedroom door at the same time he did some minutes later.

'Ah, did you get lost? Sorry about that, but I stayed to say a few explanatory words.' He opened the door and gestured for her to precede him.

'Look, you can't do this—'

'What do you think I'm going to do? Seduce you?'

'I don't *know*—'

'Then I'll tell you, Dominique,' he said precisely, and with considerable irony. 'I have this urge to kiss you at least once more, that's all. Now, we could do it out here in the passage if you prefer.' He raised an eyebrow at her.

Dominique breathed heavily, saw again the cool, utter determination in his eyes, and walked into the bedroom. But she said as he followed her and closed the door behind him, 'This is not acquiescence, just a desire to fight you in private.'

'Fight me?' he mused. 'Are you serious?' His eyes glinted wickedly.

She bit her lip then said tautly, 'I mean—try to reason you out of this madness.'

'All right.' He strolled over to one of the wing-chairs beside the fireplace, sat down, stretching his long legs out in front of him, and eyed her amusedly. 'Where should we begin?'

Dominique turned away and folded her arms across her body in an oddly protective gesture, which she didn't see him note with a faint frown. 'Why *are* you persisting when I've made it so obvious I don't want to?' she said at last, and turned back to him with shadows of weariness and effort in her eyes.

He considered briefly. 'Hurt pride? Would you buy that?' he queried.

Her lips parted and she searched his expression, but all she saw as he accepted her scrutiny was that cool indifference he did so well...

'If you think it's funny to play games with me, Mr...Rory,' she said deliberately, 'I—'

'What about the sense of *mystery* about you, then, Dominique?'

'There is no—'

'There must be,' he countered. 'While I hesitate to repeat myself, you liked it—you loved it the last time we kissed... Do I have to say any more?'

'And now I'm going to pay for that aberration,' she said huskily, and came to a sudden decision. 'All right, on one condition—that it makes us square, that it wipes everything out because I've made my reparations, and that you'll leave me in peace!'

He stood up slowly and came to stand in front of her so that she had to look up into his eyes. And she shivered inwardly both at what she saw there—the contempt—and at the undeniable frisson her whole body was experiencing at the thought of being intimate with Rory Jones again...

He said, though, 'On second thoughts, no—I think I'll leave it until you kiss me because you want to.

Which you will, Dominique. And until I find out more about why you're fighting yourself so determinedly. Goodnight. Sleep well,' he added with a lethal kind of gentleness, and walked out of the room without a backward glance.

'Yes, I see,' Dominique said the next day in the property office—a much less pretentious edifice than the homestead—where all the station accounts were kept. 'So those two properties, Mount Livingstone and Waverley Downs, interact and are owned by the same company—a family company with you now as chief shareholder. It's a good system if, as you say, Waverley Downs is much less drought-prone and you can move stock between the two, and so far as tax minimisation goes, but you could be outvoted if—'

'If the rest of them decided to gang up on me?' Rory Jones said with a grin. 'I can't see Belinda and Luke doing that.' He looked across at Luke, who was sitting in on the session.

He said briefly, 'Bel would kill me.'

'How about this...Bernard Graham?' Dominique trailed her finger down a sheet of paper. 'Who is he?'

'My cousin. His mother, now deceased, was my father's sister, and he inherited her share. He has a wife and two children.'

Something in Rory's voice made Dominique look up into his eyes. 'And?' she said.

Luke Miller stirred but said nothing.

'Well, it's not beyond the bounds of probability that Bernard would vote against me,' Rory said. 'But, as I said, without Luke and Belinda it would be a pointless exercise.'

Dominique looked down again and made a mental

note that not everything in the Jones family garden was lovely. All she said was, 'This third property you're thinking of acquiring by way of raising a mortgage...I gather you have some negative gearing in mind?'

'Yes, that's what I particularly wanted to discuss with you, Dominique,' Rory said, and added with an amused twist to his lips, 'So, you see, I didn't bring you all this way for nothing.'

'We could quite easily have discussed negative gearing on the Gold Coast...'

'Ah, but to get a rounded-out view of this family company, meeting them has to be a help.'

Dominique opened her mouth to dispute this, but noticed Luke watching with his eyes narrowed. She said instead, tonelessly, 'I suppose so.'

Rory grinned and stood up. 'Is there anything else you'd like to see here? If not I could show you around a bit more.'

'How did you sleep?'

Dominique glanced at him. They were bouncing along a rough track in a utility that was distinguished by the fact that it had its exhaust-pipe raised above the roof, which she'd had explained to her as a necessity when driving through water.

'Quite well, thank you.' It wasn't true, and she wondered if anything about her betrayed this, but beyond one searching little glance he made no further comment. 'Where are we going?'

'I thought I'd show you some stock and a bit of Sturt's Stony Desert at first hand.'

'Thanks.'

He raised a wry eyebrow. 'That prospect doesn't seem to fill you with enthusiasm.'

'It's...very hot.'

His look changed to one of concern. 'Too hot? I'm sorry—it's actually not as hot as it can get, with this bit of cloud cover today, but if you want I can turn back.'

'No, I might as well—' Dominique stopped and bit her lip.

'Get it over and done with?' he suggested drily.

She sighed and said baldly, 'Yes.'

'Dominique, I'm not an ogre,' he said evenly.

'You give a pretty good impression of it at times.'

'OK, we'll cut it short.' He changed gear and swung the wheel.

'Oh, look, no,' she said exasperatedly. 'I am interested; I'm just a bit tired.' And she flinched as this admission came out unwittingly.

He swung the wheel back but continued at a slower pace. 'I thought so.'

'Does that mean I'm looking—haggard?' she suggested with a faint smile, although why she should be amused now was a bit of a mystery to her.

'I doubt if you could,' he responded gallantly, and somehow the tension between them lessened as they rattled over a cattle-grid.

And they drove on in a fairly companionable silence until Dominique said, 'It's hard to imagine *anything* being able to survive out here, let alone cattle.'

'Nevertheless they do. There is feed, although not a lot at the moment, but of course it's never a high-density proposition—I mean per head per acre kind of thing—but there's a lot of empty country out here.'

'I believe you.' She gazed through the windscreen. 'Is this the desert?'

'The fringe of it, yes—I'll pull off the track on a bluff a bit further up and we can get out.'

*   *   *

'It's amazing,' Dominique said slowly as she gazed around.

The ground was covered with what he'd told her were gibber stones—rusty-coloured small rocks—and they stretched as far as the eye could see, but the contours of the earth weren't flat beneath the huge, cloud-streaked sky. There were barren headlands, or bluffs, as Rory called them, such as the one they were on—a legacy, he told her, of the time when the whole area had been an inland sea.

And gradually the subtle browns and ochres became plainer to her, and she sensed an aura of timelessness, an aura of space and austerity, an old, old, feeling to this desert that was a rather unique sensation.

'Do the wild flowers bloom here?' she asked, entranced despite the almost living, tangible torment of the heat as the sun came out.

'Yes, they do, although it's nothing like the splashes of colour you get around Charleville, Longreach, Quilpie and Windorah and even down to Thargomindah. In that sort of red-sand mulga country you get paper daisies, gidyeas, bluebells, Prince of Wales feathers, cassias and grevilleas and many others in plum reds, yellows, purple, mauves, white—they look like an artist's palette on the red sand. Out here they're much more discreet—tenacious little plants with tiny delicate blooms that are still a—sheer miracle.'

'A botanist's paradise, in other words,' she ventured.

He smiled. 'If you're lucky. It can be years and years between a really good showing.'

'Do you…I mean, I don't quite know how to put this, but are you a practising botanist?'

'In my spare time. I'm a consultant to several botanical gardens around the country, I *do* have a landscape-gardening firm and I'm writing a thesis on desert plants in this area at the moment. Yes, I suppose I am, amongst other things.'

'How old are you?' Dominique asked, surprising herself.

'Thirty-three. About five or six years older than you, I would estimate.'

'Six, yes.'

'Do you mind?'

'Why should I mind?' Dominique raised an eyebrow at him.

'I suppose what I'm trying to get at is your preference in men.'

'At the moment, none,' Dominique said flatly.

'All on account of this Bryce Denver? That seems a bit excessive, doesn't it?'

She opened her mouth, closed it, then said, 'I don't know. But I can't quite seem to help this allergy I possess towards good-looking, charming men.'

'Other than when you need to be made love to, that is?' he queried gravely, but she knew that he was laughing at her.

Dominique looked steadily ahead and said after a moment, 'What's that mound of stones over there, do you think?'

'Ah, end of subject! Uh—' he looked in the direction she was pointing '—an old opal prospect, I would imagine.'

'Can we have a look?'

'If you're not too hot and mind your step; these stones can be treacherous, especially in a mound.'

'Well, no opals that I can see,' she said ruefully about fifteen minutes later, and slipped on a little pile of gibbers.

He caught her, steadied her and pulled her into his arms.

'Rory,' she said unsteadily, 'I'm fine, thank you.'

'Are you? I'm not,' he murmured with that wicked glint in his blue eyes. 'I've been wondering how to engineer something like this, actually.'

Dominique compressed her lips.

'Oh, not out here, in the desert with the sun blazing down on us,' he went on softly and lazily, 'but one has to make do with whatever comes one's way, I feel.' And he ran one hand through the hot, heavy mass of her hair and the other down her back over the white cotton shirt she wore with thin beige trousers, pulling her slightly closer so that she was leaning against him.

Dominique sighed and said, 'You're being a bit juvenile, aren't you?'

'Does it *feel* juvenile to you?'

Dominique paused, trying to think of something quite damning to say, but it was a fatal error in tactics.

She became aware of his body through the thin stuff of her clothes and his khaki shirt and trousers, of the sweat trickling down between her breasts and how they felt against him. How her thighs were touching his, how he was looking down at her with those blue eyes that could be clever or cool or so amused, that could be tiger-like and oddly damning of *her*, yet now were narrowed and enigmatic although quite unamused. How his hands were roaming her back now, from her shoulder-blades to her hips—and how she could feel herself softening helplessly beneath both them and the strong, hard feel of him against her.

And instead of saying anything—anything articulate, anyway—she made a tiny, husky sound in her throat that was a strange mixture of denial, frustration and exasperation.

Whereupon he laughed quietly, kissed her lightly on the mouth and released her, although he took her hand as he guided her back to the utility. He also said, 'We'll fry if we stay out here much longer.' But he said nothing more, nor did he do anything more until they were back in the utility with the air-conditioning on, although Dominique sat in a wary sort of silence waiting for what was to come.

What came was that as they drove off he said, with a wryly raised eyebrow, 'You were saying...?'

She adjusted the grille of the air-conditioner so that it blew directly onto her face, which was hot not only from the heat outside, and answered stiffly, 'Nothing—that I was aware of.'

'Implying, then—but perhaps I can tell you—'

'Look, don't bother,' she interrupted wearily, then tensed as he grinned good-humouredly. 'I don't understand you,' she went on unwillingly, oddly compelled to speak, all the same. 'If you *could* read that I was implying—well—' She stopped and grimaced.

'A certain amount of dissatisfaction with yourself?' he suggested.

She bit her lip, couldn't deny it and remained silent.

'So why am I not—cast into the depths of despair therefore? I'll tell you why,' he said ingenuously. 'I'm like a man reborn, Dominique.'

'What—' she licked her lips and frowned '—do you mean?'

'It's quite simple—you do still like being in my arms, being held and touched—'

'How did you...?'

He looked at her briefly but that blue glance said it all, and a fresh wave of colour chased across her cheeks.

'So,' he continued, 'my faith is renewed in myself and in you. I'm a happy man, therefore, and quite content to make do with small pleasures until the larger ones—er—come round. I did tell you I wasn't an ogre, didn't I? Although...' he paused thoughtfully '...perhaps I was a bit rough on you last night.'

'You're...you *are*...' But she couldn't go on.

'Impossible? So I've been told—and also that I can be impossibly nice if I set my mind to it.'

'I'm really not interested in what other women think of you,' she murmured.

'Quite right too. It's a sentiment I share myself—or rather it's a principle I adhere to. I always like to make my own judgements, which is why I've formed no opinion yet as to why you and Bryce Denver almost but not quite got to the altar—nor have I sought any advice on the subject. But one day I will understand—you'll probably tell me yourself.'

'I don't know why you don't set yourself up as a lonely-hearts columnist,' Dominique said tartly.

'I don't either—to be the recipient of those kinds of confidences has been my lot quite frequently.'

Dominique stared at him—a look he returned quizzically—before she said in a goaded sort of voice, 'If you think I'm gong to join a long line of women who've confided in you, think again, Rory Jones.'

'We'll see,' he said placidly.

'I mean, above all it indicates an enormous ego,' Dominique marvelled. 'It's as if you're saying you're so good with women—'

'I am.'

She made a disgusted sound, but couldn't help unburdening herself further. 'It's also like saying we're some sort of inferior species; it's rather like saying you're good with horses or dogs!'

He burst out laughing.

'Are you…are you having me on?' she asked after a stunned moment.

'Only a little; I—'

'Well, how come you're unattached and fancy-free at—?'

'At the grand old age of thirty-three? The one girl I thought of marrying passed me over for someone else,' he said tranquilly.

'You don't sound particularly upset!'

'One gets over these things, although I suppose a certain wariness remains.' He shrugged.

'Are you having me on again, or is this true?' Dominique demanded.

He cast her a look that was so intensely alive and amused that she caught her breath for some reason. He said gravely, however, 'Well, well, Dominique, are you asking for an explanation of my former love life? Could this be the start of a full, frank exchange between us on the subject?'

'I…'

'I thought not,' he murmured, and his lips twisted as she clenched her hands in her lap. 'Never mind; I'm a patient man, as I told you. But *you* don't have to exist in a torment of curiosity—she married my cousin instead,' he said, and smiled sweetly at her.

Dominique's eyes widened. 'Bernard Graham?'

'None other,' he agreed. 'Who now manages Waverley Downs. I think they're fairly happy, and they have two children, as I told you, but it would probably be fair to say that Bernard and I are not and never will be the closest of cousins. Is there anything else you'd like to know?' he asked politely.

Dominique swallowed and said stiffly, 'No. I apologise if I seemed... Well...I apologise.'

'Oh, that's quite all right. I *did* get over it a long time ago.'

'But haven't found anyone since...' Dominique stopped and could have bitten her tongue off.

'That remains to be seen,' he murmured quite offhandedly. 'Now, *there* are a few specimens of a particularly drought-resistant strain of cattle,' he said casually. And he pointed.

'Is...is that why they have those big humps?' Dominique said confusedly as she tried to come to grips with what he'd said last, and thought on another level of her mind...Does he seriously mean me?

CHAPTER FIVE

IT WAS late that afternoon before she left the cool confines of her newly allocated, air-conditioned bedroom, mainly because she'd slept heavily after lunch although she'd only intended to lie down for half an hour.

It was Belinda she encountered on the veranda with a tea-tray beside her, Belinda who said brightly and with no trace in her manner of the snub she'd received from Rory the night before, 'Do join me, Dominique! Everyone else has departed. Now, what kind of tea would you like? Earl Grey? And there are some delicious little macaroons to go with it.'

'Thank you. I really need something to perk me up!' Dominique rubbed her face. 'I slept like a log, which is something I never do in the afternoons.'

'It's the heat.'

'But I should have been working.'

'Is Rory such a slave-driver?' his sister asked curiously.

'No—uh, where is he?' Dominique asked warily.

'Out with Luke. Do you need him?'

'No! No,' Dominique said hastily.

'I see.' Belinda paused and gazed at Dominique in that unnervingly frank way of hers. Then she said, 'Rory warned me on pain of death not to say another *word* to you about Bryce Denver; he was quite unpleasant about it as a matter of fact, so I won't. But—' she smiled suddenly '—I'm dying of curiosity—how well do you know Rory?'

Dominique met that frank gaze coolly and wondered if this was a roundabout way of finding out what had happened last night—possibly something else Belinda had been warned off. 'Not that well. We met at Gayle Gyngell's birthday party five or six days ago and then discovered he was a client of Conrod, Whitney & Smith.'

'So you *are* his accountant!'

'I most certainly am,' Dominique replied with some irony.

'I mean *only* his accountant. Aren't you dying to go to bed with him? Most girls are—I know Gayle was at one stage. Did you know she designed my wedding dress?'

'Yes. And mine,' Dominique said with even more irony.

'What did you do? Cut it up? I would have!'

'I believe you. No. I gave it to the local Op Shop.'

'Oh, now, that's even better,' Belinda Miller said gleefully.

'Was it from Gayle that you heard about me?' Dominique asked after a moment.

Belinda grimaced. 'Yes, but only because she was really upset for you, I think. I was down there having a fitting one day—oh, months and months ago—when she took a phone call and came back in a real rage. Not that she told me any sordid details, but she did mention both your names and said how brainy you were—an accountant and so on—and I had met Bryce, so when you showed up here yesterday I put two and two together when your name rang a bell. That's all.'

Dominique smiled suddenly. 'A woman with a past—it's really the last thing I thought I'd ever be.'

'Yes, well, they tell me men can be very difficult,

although personally I've not found it so,' Belinda mused. 'Luke certainly isn't! In fact I sometimes wish he was more like Rory, who is a very, very complex man, as Anna discovered to her cost—but then she should never have married Bernard. I don't suppose you've met her? But you will.' Belinda rested a dark, speculative gaze upon Dominique. 'If you're going to Waverley Downs on this little tour of duty, you'll meet both Anna and Bernard.'

And you don't for one minute believe that there's only business between me and your brother, do you, Belinda Miller? Dominique thought, and flinched inwardly. 'Will I?'

'Yes. Now, that should be interesting,' Belinda said thoughtfully. 'But I'll say no more.'

Dominique felt a flash of irritation and said before she stopped to think, 'He's told me about her, as a matter of fact.'

'Has he now?' Belinda murmured, and narrowed her eyes to study Dominique critically. What she would have said next, though, they were destined not to know as quick, urgent footsteps sounded through the house and a dusty man erupted onto the veranda with the news that Luke Miller had fallen off a horse and broken his arm.

There were only two of them for dinner that night: Dominique and Rory. Luke had been flown to the nearest hospital and Belinda, looking pale and grim, had gone with him. It was a multiple fracture.

And after their meal Rory said, 'Do you think you could entertain yourself for a while, Dominique? There are a few things I need to do.'

'Of course. Don't worry about me, but—is there anything I could do?'

'No, thank you,' he replied courteously.

'Then I might do some work—some of my own work.' She looked around the lamplit lounge then beyond to the dining room. 'Would you mind if I used the dining-room table?'

'Not at all. Aren't you tired?'

'No. I slept for hours this afternoon,' she said ruefully.

His gaze drifted over her. She'd changed into slim trousers and a knitted top the colour of ripe wheat and her bronze shoes. 'All right,' he said abruptly, and turned away.

Dominique worked for an hour with her papers spread all around her—the papers that Rory had provided of his affairs—then she stretched and rubbed the back of her neck and looked up to see him watching her from the doorway.

She lowered her arms, suddenly supremely conscious of how the knit material of her top was outlining her breasts. 'I didn't hear you.'

'I know. Finished?'

'Yes, I guess so.' She shuffled the papers together and put them into her briefcase.

'Would you like a nightcap?'

She hesitated briefly, but it suddenly seemed churlish to refuse. 'Thank you.'

What he brought her was an Irish coffee, and she raised a wry eyebrow at the way the cream was artistically piped on the top.

'Not me—Cook,' he said, and sat down at the other

end of the cream, linen-covered settee. The lounge was shadowy but the lamplight picked up the gleam of silver photo-frames here and there, the porcelain figures, the sheen of wood, and it turned the Persian carpet at their feet into a mysterious dark blue oriental field of creamy, scrolled arches and minarets.

'Have you heard how Luke is?'

'Yes. He's had an operation to pin the bone—he'll be fine eventually but it's going to take time.'

'Your sister was very upset—I mean, there's no reason why she shouldn't be.' Dominique gestured awkwardly and sipped her coffee.

'It's not the usual role one would ascribe to Belinda, however. Yet in her own way she's very fond of Luke. He stabilises her. I suspect she gives him hell from time to time, but it just bounces off him.'

'She said she wishes he was a bit more like you sometimes.'

'Did she?' He cast her an interrogative blue look. 'When did she say that?'

'This afternoon.' Dominique bit her lip and wished that she hadn't told him.

'How come? I mean, it seems an odd sort of conversation for you two to be having.'

'It was an odd sort of conversation all round,' Dominique replied with a slight smile. 'Thank you for warning her off Bryce Denver, by the way, but you didn't have to.'

His lips twisted. 'I was obviously not successful.'

'You were, in a way. She—er—concentrated on how well I knew you.'

'What did you tell her?'

Dominique was silent, then she looked at him with a

little shrug as if to say that there was not a lot she *could* say on the subject.

He grimaced and stretched his arm along the back of the settee, but surprised her by saying, 'What were you like as a child, Dominique? Were you an only child?'

'Yes, I was,' she said slowly. 'How could you tell?'

'I just have this mental picture of you being a—reserved, sometimes lonely little girl. I don't know why.'

'Because you see me as a reserved, sometimes lonely big girl?' she suggested, and laid her head back. 'I suppose I was. My father was a rather austere type of person and…women had a very definite place in his scheme of things. So my mother stayed very much in the background and so did I, I guess.

'She was lovely,' she said warmly, then sighed. 'But sometimes a little bit sad. I got the feeling it was because…she never could get *right* through to him.

'We always did everything so correctly,' she mused. 'I mean, he placed enormous emphasis on a quiet, ordered existence. He would have been—' she smiled ruefully '—horrified to hear of me being virtually left at the altar, but then, of course…so was I. What were you like?' she asked, turning her head to him swiftly.

He thought for a moment. 'Temperamental, always on the go, more often in trouble than out of it but, believe it or not, lonely too.'

'Because of your parents fighting all the time?'

'Probably. Because my father was so determined that I wasn't going to be ruined, life was one rigorous exercise after another, one constant fight to excel at everything one did. But I can remember,' he said quietly, 'when I was about sixteen or seventeen, desperately wanting someone to love.'

Dominique's lips parted. 'A girl?'

'Yes. But really love as opposed to dating. I wanted my own girl that I could protect and slay dragons for, who I could be quiet with and hold and cherish, and say thing to that I'd never said to anyone else—things she'd understand about my hopes and dreams and frustrations.' He paused and shrugged. 'It was as if I had this untapped reservoir of love to bestow and no one to bestow it on. It was almost like a physical ache.'

'There *must* have been girls.' Dominique studied him openly and thought that at sixteen or seventeen there would have been girls falling all over themselves for Rory Jones.

'Oh, yes,' he said with a slight shrug, and as if it didn't give him much pleasure. 'But at that age it's all so complicated—not to mention not the right time to be deeply involved with anyone,' he added wryly.

'Did you ever find anyone?'

'Well, I think one—' he paused again '—grows up, perhaps.'

Dominique didn't contest this evasion because she was curiously moved as she pictured Rory Jones as an active, extrovert, good-looking teenager, good at everything he turned his hand to but longing for love.

'I…know what you mean,' she said very quietly, then stirred as his hand moved and rested on her hair.

'Are you dying for someone to love, Dominique?'

'Not…any more. Perhaps I've grown up too.'

'I wonder,' he said meditatively, and continued before she could speak, 'So there was a time when you felt that way yourself?'

'There was a time…yes.'

'How can you be so sure it's gone?' His hand moved rhythmically on her hair.

'In light of what happened with you?' she enquired prosaically, or so she hoped.

'Yes.'

'There was a distinct reservation, nevertheless, about getting further involved with you. I thought it might have shown through.' A faint, wry smile curved her lips.

He was silent for a time and she turned to look at him eventually, moved to say involuntarily, 'What are you thinking?'

'I was wondering how to offer you a no-ties involvement. I was wondering whether I'd get my face slapped again.'

'I don't...I don't think I know what you mean,' she said slowly.

'Well, for instance, if you *do* on the odd occasion feel like some physical contact with a man why not call on me? After all, you know me now.'

A slow wave of colour coursed up Dominique's throat. 'I *was* starting to quite like you,' she said tensely.

He laughed softly. 'I'm damned with faint praise. The problem is, of course, I rather more than "like" you. It's even coming between me and my sleep.'

'You said only today that you were quite content with small pleasures,' she retorted, sharply and unwisely.

'Oh, I think we could make this a small pleasure,' he drawled, and moved closer to her. 'I'll only kiss you, if that's what you mean.'

'No it's not—look, please don't make me have to...' She trailed off and couldn't help herself. His sheer proximity, the wicked glint in his blue eyes as he regarded her with his mouth just quirking at the corners, the clean male tang of his skin, one of his beautiful hands resting lightly on her knee—all of it caused her to breathe erratically and shiver visibly, but not with distaste...

'Now, Dominique,' he said gravely, observing these things with a slight but significant lift of an eyebrow, 'you know and I know how well we do this. It's even fair to say we have great difficulty keeping our hands off each other in these circumstances, however strange, foolish, an aberration or whatever you like to call it, it is. Do you know that your mouth is like silk when I'm kissing you? And your nipples harden to little points. In case you've forgotten, let me show you.'

He did just that—put his hands on her shoulders then drew them down her to cover her breasts beneath the wheat-coloured knit of her top—and of course it happened. She felt her nipples tingle and start to unfurl, and he and she started to breathe as one as he went on to touch, hold and kiss her in a way that she couldn't deny produced a heady rapture in her.

She thought dimly that her reaction was still to do with what he'd told her about his teenage years—either that or he did it so well that one would have to be a block of wood to be unmoved, she thought in a more down-to-earth way as he lifted his head at last.

'So you see?' he murmured, his eyelids still heavy as he gazed at her mouth and his breath fanned her cheek.

'Yes, I see,' she replied huskily. 'You can be impossibly nice, it's true. But I've fallen prey to this kind of niceness once before—with disastrous consequences—'

'Did he kiss you like that?' Rory interrupted abruptly.

Dominique hesitated. 'Not exactly, no,' she said honestly after a moment.

'It didn't have quite this magic?' he persisted.

'Well...' Oh, hell, she thought; it *didn't* but...

'Then why on earth did you ever agree to marry the man?' he demanded.

That brought her right back to earth with a bump. 'It's none of your business.'

'Of course it is!' he countered.

'Well, I didn't have you to use as a yardstick, did I?' she said angrily. 'I didn't really have anyone—now there's an idea! You could set yourself up not only as a lonely-hearts columnist but as a practical consultant in these matters. Give lessons—or perhaps that's what you *do*. Send all your ex-girlfriends out—'

'Dominique,' he said amusedly, but with a distinctly dangerous look in his eyes, 'I'm coming to know that when you claw like a cat you're working from the back foot—on the defensive, in other words.'

'I'm not!'

'Oh, yes, you are, my dear, and it doesn't become you.'

'Well, what do you want me to say?' She glared at him, her green eyes alight with anger and just the suspicion of tears. 'Thank you very much, sir; that was lovely—I didn't know what I was missing out on?'

He sat back. 'No. How long are you going to hide behind that kind of thing?'

'What kind of thing?'

'The conscience-salving—I suspect—balm,' he said slowly, 'of all my ex-girlfriends—as they exist in your imagination, that is.'

'There haven't been any? Oh, come on, Rory Jones, I don't believe you.'

'Yes, there have, but I deny the implicit charge that I'm a playboy—is that what you really think I am?'

'It's a little hard not to. Your own sister told me every

girl she knows is dying to go to bed with you. Gayle Gyngell more or less told me the same thing.'

'Spare my blushes,' he said with a chuckle, and not a blush in sight. 'On the contrary, I'm very selective in that regard,' he added more soberly.

'And your modesty is overwhelming,' Dominique marvelled.

He looked amused again, but returned to the attack obliquely. 'Did you mean earlier, when you were contriving to be as insulting as you could, that Bryce Denver was your first man?'

Dominique sat up. 'I'm going to bed.'

'All right,' he said obligingly. 'But for the record, Dominique, if you're an old-fashioned girl with old-fashioned ideas on love and marriage who fell for a man who didn't quite see things your way, I do understand how frightened you are of it happening again. It's quite natural.'

Dominique went still. 'Why do you say that?' she asked uncertainly after a moment.

He didn't reply immediately but scrutinised her thoroughly with narrowed blue eyes. 'Because I've got the feeling it's true,' he said in a different voice. 'Were you too clever for your peers of the opposite sex while you were at university, for example?'

'I...' She bit her lip and looked uncomfortable.

'Were you reared towards impossibly high morals by your stiff, austere father so that even when you weren't too clever for them they thought you were cold and austere yourself, those same peers?'

She swallowed. 'I didn't sleep around, if that's what you're saying.'

He smiled rather gently. 'So tell me about Bryce Denver and how he cracked the shell—if he did.'

'If I knew that I probably wouldn't be in this mess,' Dominique replied tautly, then winced. 'That is to say—all right.' She looked at him bitterly. 'Perhaps I'm beginning to understand. Between Sally and Gayle and *you*, I'm being rather bludgeoned with it.

'He…well, he was good-looking, charming, or so I thought,' she said drily, 'and I thought I'd fallen in love, but at the same time—' she paused, then shrugged '—I wanted to do things the way my father would have wanted me to, I guess—get to know him, get engaged to him—' She stopped suddenly and looked down at her hands.

'Get married to him before you slept with him?' Rory Jones suggested. 'Have a truly white wedding, in other words?'

'Yes,' Dominique said bleakly.

'How long did he go along with all that?'

'If what I later discovered is true, he was sleeping around *while* we were engaged.'

'So—' he frowned '—why do you think he went along with it at all?'

Dominique laid her head back with a sigh. 'Do you know, he's very ambitious, Bryce, and I—well, I came into quite a bit of money when my parents died and I have to think now…that that was his main objective. With hindsight that's what *I* think at least.'

'And that's why he appeared to be content to do things as you wanted.'

'Yes.' She closed her eyes briefly. 'Although he did tell me at the end that it was only natural for him to look elsewhere for consolation, that it was all my fault, in other words… What really upsets me, I guess, is the thought that I could have been so taken in. Because I think a man who would do that to you while you're engaged would probably keep on doing it to you, whether I was right to…go for a white wedding or not.'

'Which has led you to mistrust your judgement ever since,' Rory commented.

'Possibly.' Dominique sat up. 'But it's something I can't seem to help. And something else I—have to do battle with, I guess, is those morals you mentioned earlier, that my father managed to instil in me so successfully—or disastrously, depending on which way you look at it,' she finished with some irony.

'How did your father cope with this brilliant daughter he'd begotten?'

'He was…perplexed,' Dominique said slowly, then smiled a bit wryly. 'Talking about coming from the back foot, I had him in a bit of a quandary when I was so determined to study accounting.'

'I can imagine. Did he encourage your career?'

'Only in a limited sort of way. When I graduated…fairly well—'

'Second in the state, you mean?'

'Who told you that?' She glanced at him narrowly.

'Frank Conrod. Go on.'

'Well, when I did, he congratulated me but took pains to point out that a career was always a problem for a woman.'

'And so Bryce Denver also represented a way to prove something, several things to your father,' Rory said thoughtfully, and added, 'You poor kid.'

Dominique bit her lip.

'So how *did* it get broken off?' he asked.

'I found out he was…with someone else. I was the last to know, although the subtle sort of set-downs I was getting by then should have warned me. And although I actually broke it off I somehow got landed with the left-at-the-altar tag. Oh, he did try to suggest there should be no ill-feeling between us.'

'And you haven't spoken to him since?'

'No, well, not until the other ni—' She stopped.

'The other night?' Rory hazarded. 'After he saw you with me?'

Dominique looked away.

'What did he say?'

'Well—and you should find this interesting—he also warned me about you—'

'I've never met the man!'

'Your reputation has preceded you, apparently,' she replied with irony.

'I don't know about that; I think it's much simpler, actually, and you're right—he's not too happy to think of someone else having you.'

Dominique glanced at him sideways then looked away awkwardly.

'What did you tell him?'

'I—' She pleated the antimacassar and wished fervently that she'd never embarked on this conversation. 'I'm afraid I succumbed to a rather base instinct, but that's all I'm going to say; I really am going to bed now.'

But he was laughing at her, softly and with rich enjoyment. 'You didn't, *did* you, Dominique, tell him you were wildly attracted to me or something along those lines?'

She blushed brightly and thus gave herself away completely. 'I'm sure you think that's rather a low thing to do,' she said stiffly, 'in light of—'

'My dear Dominique, on the contrary; I congratulate you! I think you did extremely well.'

'But it's not true!'

'All the same, at least it shows some spirit, and—
who knows?—one day it might be. It certainly won't
be for lack of trying on my part.'

She did stand up then and he stood up too, looked
down at her shuttered expression and said in a different,
completely sober voice, 'You are rather a mixed-up girl,
aren't you?'

Her eyes, lit with a sort of angry astonishment, flew
to his. 'I'm certainly not a child!'

'No? I wonder. I do find something oddly childlike
about you at times, but I don't think it's to be wondered
at, really. You're beautiful, brainy—which is often an
entirely different thing to being streetwise—repressed,
and definitely in need of the right man to look after you
and bring you all together. Well, goodnight, my dear.'

Dominique stared at him speechlessly, but his expression was entirely dispassionate, even sombre as he
returned her gaze. Until she made a frustrated little
sound and turned on her heel.

She woke after tossing and turning for hours then falling
into a deep sleep, feeling nearly as tired as when she'd
gone to bed, and for the second morning in a row.

What am I doing here? she wondered and answered
herself cynically. Trying not to lose my job at the whim
of a man I don't…understand, to put it mildly.

Am I so childish? she asked herself with a frown, and
stared at nothing in particular for a few minutes as she
found herself suddenly wondering what it would be like
to know a man who didn't put her down subtly, as
Bryce had towards the end and as her father had.

She got up rather suddenly then, showered and
dressed in knee-length checked beige and white shorts

and a cool white blouse, tied her hair back with a simple white ribbon and took herself to breakfast.

Rory was there ahead of her, eating bacon and eggs unconcernedly and looking fresh, rested, big, vital—and more than any woman should have to fight at this time of day, Dominique thought bitterly.

So she said the first thing that came into her head. 'What are we going to do now? I mean, with Luke and Belinda gone and floods coming will you still be able to go on with this ridiculous tour you're subjecting me to?' She helped herself to a boiled egg and sat down opposite to him.

'And how are you this morning, Miss Lindwall?' he replied mockingly. 'No, we won't be able to go on with the tour so we'll be staying here for the rest of the week.'

'I'm *not* staying here for a whole week,' Dominique said about half an hour later.

They were in the study—a beautifully panelled, book-lined room that she was, however, in no mood to appreciate. Rory Jones was lounging behind a desk and she was standing tensely at the window. There was little formal garden, as such, at Mount Livingstone, and whilst inside the homestead you could forget where you were, once you looked beyond the shrubs at the red earth that stretched to the horizon you were always reminded of the proximity of the twin deserts out there.

'Why not? I know it's not as good as showing you everything else, but I could tell you about them in a lot of detail. In fact we could work together here rather well. Forgive me, Dominique, but I can't see the difference between being here with me and being away with me.'

'Look—' she strode over to a chair in front of the desk and sat down abruptly '—would you please allow me to take my childish self back to the coast? This is only a farce—'

'I didn't say childish,' he interjected.

'Childish, childlike—there's not a lot of difference—'

'Yes, there is. Childish has connotations of being spoilt and difficult, whereas childlike, as I meant it, is being a bit naïve and old-fashioned. There's nothing wrong in it; it's just the way one is when one is...has had the pressures and influences you've had.'

Dominique stared at him. 'Do you seriously believe that?'

'What other explanation could there be for you to want to marry a man you wouldn't allow to sleep with you?'

Dominique flinched visibly and clenched her hands. 'I...I...*all right*. I admit it. I must have been quite dumb, if nothing else, but it's over—'

'I don't know about that,' he mused. 'I think it will only be over when you can forget the spectre of having to give your wedding dress to an Op Shop before the wedding.'

'Who...?' she whispered.

'Belinda. She gave me some advice when I spoke to her on the phone this morning. She told me that any girl who had gone through that needed careful, considerate handling.'

Dominique opened and closed her mouth bewilderedly several times before saying finally, 'Belinda said that?'

'She most certainly did. I told you, she's not a bad

person, my sister Belinda, just a bit overwhelming at times.'

'If you really want to know, I think you're all quite mad!'

'Now that *would* be a bit discomfiting,' he remarked, settling his shoulders negligently against the chair-back, crossing his ankle over his knee and smiling sweetly at her frustrated look. 'I mean, to discover how much you enjoyed kissing a mad man. I think even I would find that—unsettling.'

Dominique ground her teeth.

'Tell you what.' He sat forward again and propped his chin on a hand. 'Why don't you at least give me the benefit of the doubt? Instead of taking as gospel the words of—' he lifted his head and counted off his fingers '—my mad sister, your friend Gayle Gyngell—who can be *quite* mad, incidentally—and your dog-in-the-manger ex-fiancé, who wanted your money more than you,' he finished with a coolly amused look, then added, 'By the way, that's not something you can accuse me of.'

Dominique stared at him tautly.

'Of course I can always threaten you with the heavy-weights again,' he murmured, and glanced meaningfully at the phone. 'Did I tell you that Frank Conrod got in touch with me when Lancelot retired and offered his own services?'

'What's that supposed to mean?' Dominique said after a pause, and added, 'Why didn't you take him up?'

'Because I've always felt he was a bit of an old woman, actually—something he probably divined. And when he artfully contrived to let slip that there was someone new and young and quite brilliant taking over from Lancelot I decided to go for some fresh blood. No, he didn't tell me you were a girl, or your name, if that's what you're about to say. But he did assure me that what was paramount with Conrod, Whitney & Smith was my *complete* satisfaction with this new...blood.'

'You're despicable, Rory Jones,' Dominique said proudly.

'But you'll stay for the rest of the week?'

'Will you undertake to forgo what *you* so artfully term "pleasures"—small or large?' she countered coldly.

He sat back. 'I don't think I can guarantee that.'

'Then I can only guarantee to stay while you do.'

His lips twisted. 'Dominique, you can't just walk off Mount Livingstone.'

'When I make up my mind to leave here, I will do so somehow or other,' she said evenly.

'Bravo,' he murmured, but his eyes mocked her again with that tiger-like look.

Good, Dominique thought. Let's see if we can keep it that way—and it was only later that she stopped to think that she couldn't recall being in such a temper for years.

CHAPTER SIX

DOMINIQUE saw nothing of Rory Jones until dinnertime that day, which allowed her to do a lot of work and, when she'd finished, to take herself on a tour of the public rooms of the homestead.

She discovered quite a few paintings by the same artists, signed 'C. Jones', that interested her particularly—not only for their charm but their subjects. Mostly they were paintings of wild flowers and the desert, but there were also some portraits of Rory and Belinda as children. It was one of Rory that captured her attention, to the extent that as she passed it on her way to dinner that evening she stopped to look at it again.

He had been twelve, according to the plate on the frame, but even then, she thought, you could see the essence of Rory Jones emerging... You could see, for example, the germ of that very assured, indifferent aura as he sat on his horse looking as if he owned the world. You could also see the daredevil streak in him, the look of a boy who might do things just for the hell of it...

She caught her breath as she studied the painting intently and thought, Does that sum up why he's doing this to me—just for the hell of it?

'Dominique?'

She started, and turned to find Rory Jones at her shoulder, looking down at her quizzically.

She coloured, of course, and would have loved the earth to open up and swallow her, but again, of course, it didn't. And, to make matters worse, she said hastily, 'Whoever painted these was very good.'

'Very good,' he agreed. 'It was my aunt.'

'Well, I suppose it's dinnertime,' she went on lamely.

'You suppose right,' he said gravely. 'May I escort you in?' And, so saying, he took her hand and led her towards the dining room. 'By the way, we could spend a few hours working tonight, if you like. I was tied up all day today, unfortunately—or perhaps not so,' he said with a considering glance.

'What's that supposed to mean?' she murmured distractedly, conscious more of the feel of her hand in his—and her seeming inability to withdraw it.

'I thought it might have given you some time to regain your equilibrium.'

'It did,' she replied briefly, and withdrew her hand.

Dominique rubbed the back of her neck and yawned. But she smothered it immediately and said, 'Yes, well, I am getting the hang of it all.'

It was ten o'clock and they'd spent the last few hours in the study, going over in detail all the companies he either owned or was a shareholder in. 'You really need your own accountant to…bring it all together. Have you thought of setting up a holding company?'

'It was what I urged my father to do quite a few years ago, but he was such a law unto himself…' He grimaced and gestured.

'Perhaps that's where you get it from. So—' she frowned '—a lot of this is quite new to you?'

'Until he died a couple of months ago, I spent most of my time on my ruling passion—he was extremely difficult to work with, you see.' He smiled.

'But you must have had *some* interest. And surely he would have wanted you to be groomed to take over?'

'Oh, I was interested, and I spent years being groomed to take over. But it never quite came to the point when he could bring himself to hand much over—I'm sure it's a problem all the time with heirs apparent.'

Dominique raised her eyebrows and had to smile herself. 'You don't sound a very loving family if you'll forgive me for saying so.'

'At times, no. But—' he sat back and laced his hands behind his head '—do you now see, Dominique, that I'm not altogether wasting your time?'

'Yes, I do,' she said thoughtfully. 'Which brings me back to my original suggestion—why don't you form a holding company to gather all the threads in with a permanent accountant?'

'If I did, would you come and work for me?'

Her eyes widened. 'You're not serious?'

'Indeed I am.'

'But...' She trailed off incredulously.

'I can guarantee it would be a good career move for you.'

Dominique glanced down the list of companies involved, the sheer wealth and complexity represented, and couldn't disagree. 'But...' she said again. 'I mean...' Again she stopped, nonplussed.

He grimaced. 'Do you mean, how would we work together?'

'Well, yes.' She stared at him, her green eyes wide and confused.

He sat forward. 'We'd have to sort out—certain things first, of course. Such as whether you can continue to be so determined to have no personal truck with me.'

She licked her lips and swallowed.

'Because, of course, if that was a problem,' he continued, 'it wouldn't work.'

'Why should it be a problem?' she said, and regretted the words as soon as they left her tongue.

'I wondered if the way you were studying my aunt Chattie's portrait indicated a tormented but undeniable sense of intrigue on your part, that's all.'

Their gazes locked fast—for the life of her Dominique couldn't seem to tear hers away. Nor could she help breathing unsteadily, but she did say, '*Are* you doing this just for the hell of it?'

His blue gaze narrowed. 'Why don't you take the few steps required to find that out, Dominique?'

'You mean...go to bed with you?'

'Yes. Because, whatever happens between us, it will never be as damaging to you as what Bryce Denver did—'

'How do you *know* that?'

'Because it would be something you want to do, it would be honest, it would be *living* life as opposed to planning it and making it something orderly and sterile—it could even make Dominique Lindwall become a warm, breathing, real woman, not a calculating machine.'

She closed her eyes then got up jerkily and stumbled out of the study.

'Why are we doing *this*?' she said tensely the next morning.

'I thought a little flight might soothe your nerves,' Rory Jones said blandly. 'I also want to see how the flood is progressing at first hand. We'll have lunch at Birdsville.'

'My nerves are fine,' she retorted.

But all he said, though with irony, was, 'Good, then this will make you positively lyrical.'

To which she responded with a cool, taut look.

'That's…all there is to Birdsville?' she said about an hour later as they flew over it.

'Yes. About a hundred and twenty souls, a pub, a vital medical outpost and not a lot else. Well, there's the racecourse.' He pointed. 'That accounts for about six thousand souls over a couple of days every September.'

'Six *thousand*. Where do they put them all?' Dominique asked as she gazed down at the speck on the brown landscape that was the famous town of Birdsville.

'They camp. Along the banks of the Diamantina, under their planes on the airstrip—wherever it's possible. It's probably one of the most famous race meetings in the country. It has, to date, a hundred-and-eleven-year unbroken history—and, of course, a lot of the proceeds go to the Flying Doctor Service.'

'It's amazing! I can't visualise it.'

'Picture one big party, a quarter of a million cans of beer, a sea of akubra and stetson hats, three hundred light planes on the airstrip, tourist types in bright colours, who come from everywhere by coach, as well as the less colourful outback types in boots and broad leather belts; picture a boxing tent, sideshows, food vendors, four-wheel drives of every description—and you have Birdsville at the races.'

Somehow, she thought, his words brought those images to mind, and she smiled at him, marvelling.

'That's the first time you've smiled at me today,' he commented.

'This is quiet something, though. What will it be like today?'

'The pub could be deserted. In between times it's only the locals and road-train drivers shipping stock who are in the area. That's Bedourie, thataway. That's Betoota over there, even smaller than Birdsville, but they both have their own racecourse, and that—' he gestured '—roughly, is the Birdsville Track. Made famous in days gone by when cattle were walked along it to the rail-head at Marree in South Australia—that's about a five-hundred-kilometre walk.'

'And it's all Flynn of the Inland Mission country.'

'Yes—there are a couple of books about him at home. I'll find them for you when we get back. Right, if you've seen enough, we'll go and have lunch.'

'1884!' Dominique said wonderingly as she stood in the blinding heat outside the single-storeyed, old-fashioned little Birdsville Hotel.

'Mmm...' Rory took her elbow and guided her up onto the pavement that ran around the pub. Their plane was parked just across the road. 'Very handy now—as it was then, no doubt. How does an ice-cold beer sound to you?'

Dominique laughed. 'I hate to be a dampener but I loathe beer. An ice-cold cola, though—now that would go down well.'

'So you see—was I right about your nerves?' he said after they'd taken off again.

'Oh—yes,' she conceded wryly. 'They are feeling much better. Is that Mount Livingstone?'

'No, it's another station.'

'They all look alike from the air.' She turned to him impulsively. 'Thanks for today.'

'My pleasure. I wish there was a lot more I could show you. It seems to bring out the best in us.'

Dominique was silent for a while. 'Do I really appear tormented to you?'

He turned his head and regarded her thoughtfully. 'Sometimes—why?'

She shrugged. 'It's not the way one likes to think of oneself, I suppose.'

'Dominique, do you ever let yourself think back to that first night?'

'I can't help—' She stopped abruptly.

He smiled drily. 'Neither can I—if it's any help.'

'Not a lot.' She turned her head to look out of the window.

'Never mind,' he consoled her. 'That's my last bait for the day. Even confirmed playboys such as myself,' he said cheerfully, 'take breaks. Now, that is Mount Livingstone—' He stopped and swore.

'What?'

'We have visitors.'

Dominique peered down to see another light plane on the runway. 'Do you know who?'

'Yes. Bernard Graham.'

'Oh.'

'Well, you'll get to meet him at least.'

'You really don't like him, do you?'

He glanced at her briefly and she was surprised at the coldness of his eyes. 'No.'

He said no more as he concentrated on landing the plane—and, as it turned out, it wasn't only Bernard Graham she got to meet but his wife Anna as well.

*   *   *

'We thought you might need some help, Rory,' Bernard Graham said as they came face to face in the homestead. 'What with Belinda and Luke out of action, Anna said we should come and see—didn't you, my love?'

Anna Graham stirred from her contemplation of Dominique and said coolly, 'How do you do? Belinda mentioned that you're Rory's accountant.' She turned to Rory. 'If we're unwelcome in any way, do tell us.'

Wonderful tawny hair like a river of silk, grey eyes with dark lashes, a stunning figure and the confident walk of a supermodel, and that same born-with-a-silver-spoon aura as Belinda and Rory themselves made Anna Graham probably the most beautiful woman she'd seen, Dominique thought as she returned the greeting mechanically—and she was as disbelieving of the accountant theory as anyone else.

'Where are the kids?' Rory said, ignoring all else.

'Left them at home—we thought we'd have a few days' break from them. Look, do you mind or don't you?' Anna said straightly.

'Dear Anna,' Rory responded, 'why should I mind?' And his blue eyes were quite charmingly disarming, if one hadn't come to know that hint of steel behind them. 'It'll be very interesting for Dominique to get to know you. Both,' he added.

'Is something wrong?' Dominique asked at dusk, coming upon the housekeeper, a friendly soul, surveying the dinner table with an expression of gloom. 'It looks rather lovely to me.' The long oak table was set with a white dinner service, yellow napkins and place mats, silver candlesticks and piled fruit in a beautiful crystal bowl in the centre.

'I hope so, but—it's just when Mrs Anna is here I get a bit nervous. She's very...stylish.'

'Four, five. I thought there were only four of us?' Dominique commented, rather than commenting on Anna Graham.

'The pastor is coming as well. He drove in on his way to Markwell Hill station and Rory persuaded him to stay the night. He's a lovely man—did you know Mount Livingstone is *famous* for its hospitality, Miss Lindwall? My mother, who worked here before me, can remember them entertaining the governor of the day, premiers, politicians and poets!'

'You certainly do things beautifully,' Dominique said sincerely.

'Well, things did slide a bit after Rory's mother died, but Belinda is very keen to restore it all to its former glory. Of course, by rights, Rory's wife should be in charge, and I sometimes wonder how Belinda will feel about that— Oh, dear! I don't know what got into me, talking my head off like this; it must be Mrs Anna again. I'll say no more!'

'Say no more about me do you mean?' Anna Graham said from the doorway, and strolled into the room. She was already dressed for dinner in a beautifully cut lime-green silky gilet over matching, pyjama-style pants and she looked groomed, poised, beautiful—and angry. 'I should hope not—to a virtual stranger.' And her grey eyes challenged Dominique.

But while the housekeeper fled in red-faced confusion Dominique refused to be cowed. 'If you're imagining I was pumping the housekeeper, you're wrong,' she said, quietly but coolly. 'And if you'll excuse me I'll get dressed for dinner.'

* * *

'Well, Lizzie Collins,' she addressed her dress as she slid it off the hanger, 'you'll have to make another appearance, because I refuse to be daunted by Anna Graham—in the matter of clothes or anything else. I wonder what on earth *did* happen between those two—' She broke off her murmured conversation with herself and her dress and bit her lip.

'Gayle Gyngell?' Anna Graham said, with narrowed eyes and an oddly penetrating look when Dominique joined them in the lounge.

'As a matter of fact, no—do you know Gayle as well?'

'As well?' Anna Graham eyed Dominique over the rim of her sherry glass, still with that odd spark of— was it interrogation in her eyes? Bernard Graham was standing beside his wife, and Rory and the pastor had not made their appearances as yet.

'Belinda asked me if this was one of Gayle's when I wore it a couple of nights ago,' Dominique said by way of explanation.

'I do know Gayle, as a matter of fact,' Anna said coolly. 'And Bernard has met Bryce Denver.' She said no more but the implication in her grey eyes was that Dominique was to be pitied as being a bit strange to have been left at the altar by someone like Bryce Denver.

'Ah, well, you know all about *me*, then,' Dominique replied offhandedly. 'It's a small world, isn't it?'

'True,' Anna Graham conceded.

'There you all are,' Rory said, coming up behind Dominique with a short, jolly-looking man in tow whom he introduced as the pastor. 'I've been told,' he added charmingly, 'that Cook is getting a bit paranoid—

soufflés are apparently difficult things to keep hanging around. Shall we go in?' And he offered Dominique his arm.

And so dinner got under way—on the surface, a leisurely, cultured meal, but beneath the surface almost tangible cross-currents were evident.

Bernard Graham revealed a faintly sardonic manner. He was dark, tall and conventionally good-looking, resembling his cousin Belinda more than his cousin Rory, but he also exhibited that indelible stamp of the Jones family, that unfailing air of confidence that a wealthy, old family background brought and Dominique knew that Bernard Graham must be wealthy in his own right.

But there wasn't the quick wit that Rory possessed, there wasn't the vitality, that magnetic *personality*, Dominique thought, that made Rory irresistible at times.

As to relations between Bernard and Anna, while there was little outward warmth there was quite a lot of talk about their children and their lives on Waverley Downs—both humorous and to do with the weather, cattle et cetera. What there was also was the odd, challenging remark that Bernard made to his wife which she simply ignored.

So why had Anna, who was both witty, worldly and intelligent, who had stunning looks and an inherent ease of manner, taken a husband who needed to be on the defensive? Taken second best in other words...? And why, having done so, and two children later, did she still bear towards Rory Jones a latent hostility that she couldn't quite hide? Not to mention a latent hostility towards any woman who was with him, she thought, still smarting from the Bryce Denver mention.

And, she wondered, was there something that she couldn't quite put her finger on beneath the cool, cul-

tured surface of Anna Graham—some hint of steel
or…some elusive *something* that didn't altogether fit,
some suggestion of more than cool, clever hostility,
something more turbulent? I don't know, she thought
frustratedly. And do they always have this insidious,
really rather appalling sort of tension going on whenever they're all together?

By the time the fruit and cheese had been served,
Rory, lounging at the head of the table, seemed to be
the only one, apart from the pastor, completely at his
ease. He was successfully smothering his dislike of
Bernard in a smooth flow of small talk, and smothering
anything other than casual geniality towards his
cousin's wife whilst trading anecdote for anecdote with
the pastor.

She watched as he peeled and quartered an apple,
then she looked up and noticed that Anna was watching
those long, beautiful hands too.

She might even have continued to think that all was
successfully smothered if she hadn't come across him
on the darkened veranda when the party had split up
quite a bit later to retire for the night.

He was standing so still that she was almost upon
him before she realised it. Standing with his hands
shoved into his pockets, staring into the night.

'Oh! I'm sorry,' she murmured as she all but bumped
into him. 'I didn't see you.'

'Well, well,' he drawled. 'My beautiful accountant
who refuses to be anything else.' And she was shocked
to see the glitter of mockery in his eyes, far more scath-
ing than anything she'd seen before.

'What—?' She stopped and licked her lips.

'You were saying?' He raised an eyebrow at her.

'I was going to say, What brought that on?'

He paused, then murmured with soft satire, 'My undoubted desire for a woman tonight, Dominique.'

Shock held her rigid for a moment. Then she said, 'Why did you ever let her go if that's how you feel?'

'I didn't say that,' he countered.

'It seems to…make sense, nevertheless.'

'What is sense?' he murmured with a wryly lifted eyebrow. 'There are times when you don't make a lot of sense, Miss Lindwall.'

Dominique hesitated, then went to turn away, but he caught her wrist. 'Don't try to kiss me out here,' she warned agitatedly.

His shockingly cynical blue gaze slid down from her gold-streaked tied-back curls to the hollows at the base of her throat, where a pulse beat erratically, to the outline of her breasts beneath the black georgette. 'Does that mean to say you have somewhere more suitable in mind?'

'*No.* I…mean—' She stopped.

'Such as coming away with me first thing tomorrow morning?' he continued, unperturbed. 'Somewhere where just the two of us could fight this out to some kind of a conclusion, sensible or otherwise and, if nothing else, *honest*?

'Or are you going to carry the fact that I can make you tremble with desire and make you kiss me with longing—carry it locked away in your heart in the hopes that it will all go away one day? You know, it might never happen this way for you again.'

'As…she's never happened for *you* again?' Dominique whispered, unable to deny his charges, suddenly unable not to have a picture in her mind of Rory Jones as a teenager, looking for someone to love, even though now he was a such a dangerously attractive man.

'I told you—' his hand left her wrist and he traced the outline of her mouth curiously gently '—I never said that.'

Her shoulders slumped suddenly when she thought of something else. She thought of Anna Graham and her unspoken implication of pity, which, without its other overtones, was, of course, what she'd seen a lot of in the last nine months. She thought of Bryce's phone call... 'Do you mean,' she said suddenly, 'not to work—just to go away together for a couple of days?'

'Yes.'

'Well, I couldn't make any promises; I mean...I don't know exactly *what* I mean!' Her eyes were suddenly shadowed with frustration.

'But you'll come?'

'Oh... How could you leave, though?' she asked, thinking of Luke, who was still in hospital but recovering well apparently, and of the flood she'd seen only that morning, creeping down the channels of the Cooper and the Diamantina.

'Bernard can take over now he's here.' Rory smiled, but it was an oddly merciless little smile. 'That's how.'

'Well...'

'Just say yes, Dominique,' he advised. 'For once in your life—since we've known each other, that is—just say yes.'

'Where are we going?'

The sun had barely crept over the horizon as the plane gained height, and no one had come to see them off—she wondered if anyone even knew they'd left.

'Uh…Noosa, I thought,' he murmured, scanning the instrument panel. 'Ever been there?'

'Of course. It's only a couple of hours' drive from the Gold Coast. But not actually to stay.'

'Good,' he said promptly.

'Why?'

'Why what?'

'Why is that good?' Dominique said with mocking patience, which was probably induced by another difficult night.

'No ghosts for me to have to deal with on top of everything else.'

She was silent. And for once so was Rory Jones for the most part, other than to point out landmarks of interest.

They landed at Maroochydore Airport, in the middle of the Sunshine Coast, which stretched as far as Caloundra in the south, and Noosa Heads to the north. He arranged to store the plane and hired a car as well as booking their accommodation. Then he took her hand and led her towards the red Ford, saying drily, 'Come, Dominique, this is supposed to be a little holiday, not a wake.'

'Like it?'

Dominique looked around the suite. She'd heard about Netanya at Noosa Heads as being an up-market, luxurious place to stay, and saw that it lived up to all expectations.

It was right on the beach, overlooking Laguna Bay and what they called the 'Paris' end of Hastings Street, and Hastings Street of Noosa was renowned for its elegant shopping and many delightful indoor/outdoor restaurants, while still retaining its low-rise, village atmosphere.

The steep, wooded national park formed one arm of the bay and the beach curved round to the mouth of the Noosa River—a protected beach with gentle, rolling surf fringed with coconut palms and banksia trees.

Their third-floor suite had the bedroom separated from the lounge by a waist-high room-divider cabinet with television, compact-disc player and video machine built in. Sliding louvred doors could close the rooms off completely from each other and more sliding glass doors opened onto a tiled, private terrace directly above the pool. The whole suite was elegantly fitted out with a thick mushroom carpet and cool tiles, broad, sumptuous couches, a small kitchenette—and a king-size bed in the bedroom, whilst in the marble bathroom there was a spa-bath quite big enough for two.

It struck Dominique as she looked around that it was a cool, elegant and very private retreat. 'It's nice,' she said. 'Shall I unpack?'

'Not yet,' he murmured.

'Rory—'

'No, Dominique, don't say a word.' And he took her in his arms.

When they stopped kissing a few minutes later she was breathless, her eyes unfocused and her mouth crushed. But he didn't let her go entirely; he cupped her shoulders and held her body against the length of his and turned his attention to the smooth column of her neck.

'You taste of sun-ripened peaches,' he murmured.

'Do I? I don't know why,' she said shakily as he undid the top buttons of her blouse so that he could slide his hands beneath it to the satiny curves and hollows at the base of her throat, and lower.

Then he simply took the blouse off, so that she was standing in her jeans and bra, and she didn't resist because she was thinking, If I *am* going to do this, let me do it now while I have the courage, *if* I am...And she tensed slightly but made no attempt to retreat.

It seemed after a few moments that Rory Jones had other ideas, though. 'Much as I'm enjoying this,' he said barely audibly, spanning her ribcage with his hands then drawing his thumbs across her nipples beneath the fine net and silky pleated material of her white bra, and watching what he was doing until he lifted his eyes to hers suddenly, 'I think we could be more relaxed about it.'

'What do you mean?'

'Let's go for a swim first.'

Dominique rocked on her feet slightly and touched him with her hands for the first time; she put them on his arms to steady herself. 'I didn't bring a costume.'

He brought his hands up to the nape of her neck and lifted her hair up. 'Such lovely, heavy hair.' Then he added in a different tone, 'You're in the best place to remedy that.'

'I...suppose so.'

'Then, should we go shopping, have a light lunch, a swim, and see how that affects us?' His eyes were very blue and she could feel the smooth muscles of his upper arms beneath his rolled-up shirtsleeves.

'Why not?' she said, but slowly and rather diffidently.

'Tell me what you're thinking, Dominique.'

'I don't really know.'

'Will it be such a momentous step? Sleeping with

me?' He lowered his hands and linked them behind her hips.

She considered, and felt his breath on her face as he kissed her brow lightly. 'I don't know—and I don't know if that's what I'm going to do. I told you, no promises.'

He lifted his head and frowned down into her eyes. 'What about doing it because you *want* to?'

'Well, there may not be much doubt about that, but—'

'Thank you, Dominique,' he said a shade drily.

She took a breath as she saw that tiger-like look fleetingly in his eyes, and said after a moment, 'Have I hurt your feelings?'

'I wouldn't put it quite like that,' he replied thoughtfully, but released her, picked up her blouse from the floor and handed it to her.

She looked at it in her hands then slipped her arms into it and started to button it up. 'Something I said has...' She shrugged.

'Offended me?' he supplied. 'Don't give it a moment's thought. Let's just go shopping. Here, let me help,' he added gravely. 'You've got it crooked.'

She opened her mouth then closed it futilely and submitted to his ministrations.

'All proper and correct, Miss Lindwall,' he drawled. 'Unless you'd like to repair your make-up? You look—' he raised a wry eyebrow '—as if you've just been thoroughly kissed.'

Once again Dominique opened her mouth, but she shut it, looked around for her bag and walked as calmly as she was able into the bathroom with it. It was not much consolation to discover that she did look—well, dishevelled, anyway.

But as she brushed her hair and tied it back, put some lipstick on and tucked her blouse in properly she was thinking that if she'd introduced a discordant note to Rory Jones's plans, she couldn't be altogether blamed, surely?

CHAPTER SEVEN

'THIS looks nice.'

'It does,' Dominique agreed, and added the costume to the three that she had already selected from the rack. She wasn't sure whether Rory was doing it to annoy her but he'd certainly got the salesgirl in the exclusive boutique that sold resort wear and lingerie into quite a flutter as he gave his utmost attention to choosing a swimsuit. 'I'll try these on.'

'Yes, do that, Dominique,' he said seriously, but with a wicked glint in his eyes.

'You're not expecting me to—?'

'Parade in them all before me? Perish the thought,' he said in shocked tones, then laughed as she tightened her mouth. 'No. Tell you what I'll do—I didn't bring anything to read so I'll nip across to that bookshop. I'm sure you're quite capable of choosing a costume. And if I'm not there when you're finished I'll be getting us a table at Aromas for lunch. How would that suit you?'

'Very well,' Dominique said coolly, and turned towards the fitting rooms as a chattering party of middle-aged women entered the shop.

'I'll take this one, thank you,' she said to the assistant some time later.

'Oh, it is lovely!' the girl said enthusiastically as she held up the soft jade Lycra one-piece. 'Goes with your eyes, and, do you know, I have just the hat to go with it—a sunhat, I mean!' And she produced a woven raffia hat with an upturned brim and a scarf tied round it in the same jade.

'Well...' Dominique hesitated.

'It gets awfully hot on the beach,' the girl said temptingly.

'Yes, you're right. I'll take it.' Dominique smiled back at her and reached for her purse.

'Oh, no! It's all paid for!'

'What do you mean?' Dominique said slowly.

'The gentleman,' the girl said warmly and with an envious sigh. 'I'll just pop the costume in with the others—there.' And she wrapped it in tissue-paper and added it to the large, elegant carrier bag that bore the boutique's name.

'*What* others?'

'Oh, would you like to see them?' The girl's eyes widened. 'Of course, I didn't think of that. But I must say he has lovely taste,' she added with another sigh, and withdrew three items from the bag, all wrapped in tissue-paper, and unwrapped them eagerly—a fine white lawn sarong, self-patterned with shadowy flowers, an exquisite ivory satin nightgown with tiny straps that crossed over the very low-cut back and with a lace panel down the front, a minuscule white bikini and a stunning, sleeveless pearl-coloured silk cocktail dress as light as air. 'They're the right size,' the girl said eagerly, 'and I'm sure they'll all look fabulous on you!'

Dominique swallowed and looked across at the bookshop, but there was no sign of Rory. 'He couldn't have known how much the costume *I* chose would be,' she said with some difficulty. 'Or about this hat.'

'Oh, he gave me an imprint of his credit card and signed it so all I have to do is add the amounts to the others!'

'I...see.'

'You are lucky,' the girl then confided. 'He's so nice, as well as—well, you know what I mean!'

Dominique approached Café Aromas and saw Rory sitting at a pavement table reading a paper, but he got up as she arrived and pulled out a chair for her.

'Dominique,' he murmured as their gazes caught, then he looked at the carrier bag and back into her eyes. 'You don't mind?' he added. 'I like the hat very much, by the way.' She was carrying the hat.

She sat down and placed the bag carefully on another chair. Then she said casually, 'Could we talk about blackmail?'

'We could if you really think it's appropriate.'

And odd spark of amusement lit her eyes. 'Well, the nightgown at least, beautiful as it is, did seem to have a touch of that about it.'

'I'm afraid I succumbed to a purely male impulse,' he said, his blue eyes regretful—or, more accurately, a complete parody of regretfulness. 'I couldn't help trying to picture you in it. And I chose the dress to go with that pair of bronzy shoes you've worn a couple of times.'

'Yes, well—' Dominique took a deep breath '—you don't also think you might have been trying to make me—come from the back foot?'

'Are you?' he queried seriously.

'For whatever sin I committed before we embarked on this shopping expedition?'

Blue eyes gazed into ironic green ones, then he said wryly, 'I wouldn't call it a sin exactly.'

'But did you honestly think buying me these things

would send me into transports of sheer delight?' she persisted.

'Ah.' He sat back and regarded her with keen appreciation and amusement. 'No, I didn't, actually. I even wondered whether you would accept them or whether you would leave them lying *spurned* upon the counter.'

She stared at him with her green eyes suddenly narrowed and arrested. Then she said with a frown, 'So, if it wasn't a sex-and-shopping kind of gesture, why are you trying to antagonise me, Rory?'

His gaze sobered, and after a moment he said consideringly, 'I'm not. But I'd rather we didn't make heavy weather of it. Believe me, there is no need.'

Dominique flushed. 'You mean you'd like it to be all light-hearted, no regrets—that kind of thing? I don't think I'm made that way,' she said honestly. 'I—'

'I don't want that either,' he countered. 'I just want you to relax and not feel as if you're making any momentous, courageous decisions. I certainly don't want it to be merely an exercise in "sex and shopping", as you put it so brutally—'

'Then—'

'Some fun along the way never hurt anyone, Dominique,' he said gently. 'Ah—here's our lunch.'

'You mean you ordered for me?'

'I was afraid you would take refuge in a Caesar salad,' she said gravely.

She cast him a speaking look. 'So you went the opposite way and ordered a hamburger with the lot and chips?'

'And a glass of wine; we did miss breakfast.'

'You're...'

But he laughed at her. 'Go on, I dare you to enjoy

it, Dominique; we are, after all, on a holiday—of some kind. By the way, are you a reader?'

'Yes, I love it, but look—'

'Joanna Trollope?' He pulled a book from a packet.

'I…no, I haven't read it.' Dominique couldn't quite hide the gleam of interest in her eyes.

'Good, I got it for you.'

'What did you get for yourself?' she enquired despite herself, and, also despite herself, ate a chip as the tantalising aroma of the hamburger wafted up to make her realise that she was indeed hungry.

'Frederick Forsyth,' he replied with a grin.

'Very manly,' she commented, and ate another chip.

'How was that?'

'Lovely.' Dominique sat back with a sigh and finished her wine. 'Not, however—' she glanced at him ruefully '—conducive to frolicking in the surf. I feel like a nice long sleep.'

'Done,' he said promptly. 'You can have the bedroom and I'll kip on one of those sumptuous settees.'

'Are you serious?'

'Perfectly! A siesta after lunch is a very civilised custom, especially in the sub-tropics. We can have our swim later.'

But she lay awake for a while, pondering their curious conversation at lunch, probing for the implications to little avail, then slept deeply and dreamlessly for an hour and a half, and when she woke he was on the terrace in a pair of board shorts, bare feet and no shirt, reading his book.

'Oh.' He looked up as she stood in the doorway rubbing her eyes. 'Feeling better?'

'No, I feel awful,' she murmured.

He put down his book. 'Then go and put your new togs on and come for a swim.'

So she changed into the jade swimsuit but tied the white sarong around her waist, and he made no comment as they left the suite and walked downstairs past the pool onto the beach.

'It was a bright, hot day and the water sparkled invitingly, and, though still with nothing said between them, they nevertheless were of one mind—apparently. Because without further ado she dropped the sarong over a rock and they waded into the water together, Dominique gasping slightly at the first refreshing chill of it, then dived into the surf.

'How was *that*?' he asked as they came out half an hour later.

'Glorious,' she murmured, picking up her towel.

'You're a good swimmer, Dominique.'

'I love it. So are you.'

'What would you like to do now? Sunbake for a while?'

'No, I'd like nothing so much as a brisk walk up the beach and then—' her mouth dimpled at the corners '—a good old-fashioned cup of tea.'

'You can have Assam or…English breakfast,' he called to her, back in the suite.

'Seeing as it's half past four in the afternoon, Assam,' she called back. She'd unpacked, showered and slipped on a pair of white shorts and a buttercup-yellow T-shirt and was wrestling with her hair in the bathroom.

'At your service, ma'am,' he said from much closer, and his reflection loomed up behind her in the mirror. 'A problem?'

She looked ruefully at her comb.

'It always looks wonderful.'

Dominique grimaced. 'Thanks.' But when she looked up his eyes weren't meeting hers in the mirror. He was looking down at her instead, and she felt a little frisson because he still wore only his board shorts and his tall body was beautifully made, and she was reminded of how it had cleaved the water with grace and power, and because, whichever way you looked at it, Rory Jones was the kind of man who could take your breath away...

'Dominique?'

'Oh.' She blinked confusedly as their gazes met in the mirror. 'I was thinking, that's all,' she said hastily. 'Well, I can do no better—' she put the comb down and turned '—so you'd better lead me to this tea.'

'It's ready and waiting on the terrace,' he murmured, but didn't move immediately. And they simply stared at each other for a long moment, then he dropped his eyes and moved aside for her to pass.

'When we go out to dinner tonight,' he said idly as they lazed on the terrace while the sun set, 'will you wear my dress?'

'Where will we go?' Dominique said after a moment.

'Palmer's is across the road. It's very nice and quite suitable for a dress like that.'

'All right. You've seen my only other dress a couple of times now.'

He smiled. 'The one that's *not* Gayle Gyngell?'

'Yes... Do they know?'

'The mob back at Mount Livingstone? I left a note for them.'

'What sort of a note?'

'Well, I didn't say we'd run off into the wild blue yonder together,' he said with an amused quirk of his lips. 'Just that I could be contacted via my secretary in Brisbane.'

'It might have given them that impression, all the same,' Dominique remarked.

'Do you care? I don't.'

'I know *you* don't—'

'Dominique—' he held up a hand and laughed '—let me rephrase. Only I don't know how to. Uh—it really has nothing to do with any of them—put it like that.'

She shrugged. 'I suppose you're right.'

'I am. Would you be happy out here on your own for a while?'

She raised an eyebrow. 'Are you going somewhere?'

'Only inside to make a few calls—business calls.'

'Yes, I'll be fine. I'll start my book.'

So she read for a while, and watched the people on the beach in between times. There were quite a few families with young, pre-school-age children—it wasn't school-holiday time—and a group of older children who must have been locals and were being trained as part of a surf club.

Then as the dusk grew Rory brought out two tall, frosted glasses of what he called a 'sundowner' mixture that was a secret recipe of his.

Dominique sipped hers and it was delicious, as she told him.

'Thank you. I've made our dinner reservations but we still have nearly an hour. Luke, you'll be happy to know, was released from hospital today.'

'Oh, yes! Is he going back to Mount Livingstone?'

'No. Belinda's taking him to the Gold Coast for a few weeks. He'll be in plaster for a couple of months.'

'To the Sheraton?' Dominique hazarded.

He shook his head. 'We have a house at Paradise Waters.'

'Why don't *you* stay there?'

'I loathe rattling around in it on my own, although I do often. But if it's a short trip it seems simpler to put up at a hotel.'

'Paradise Waters,' Dominique said slowly. 'So it's probably a minor mansion?'

He grimaced. 'My father built it.'

'How many other homes are there round the country?' she asked gently.

'Only one other, in Brisbane. Now, *it's* nice—old and comfortable and overlooking the river. Where do you live?'

She told him.

'Do you own the apartment?'

'Yes—by courtesy of what my parents left me. They were killed in an accident a couple of years ago.'

'So you're on your own?'

'Well, no close relatives.'

He smiled across at her rather warmly and she smiled back, and they sat in a companionable silence until he suggested that she start to get dressed.

The dress was straight, short and sleeveless, and her bronze shoes did go well with it. So did the slight glow that the sun had given her skin, and the added highlights it had given to her hair, which she tamed and wound into a pleat.

'Ready?'

'Ready,' Dominique agreed, and added involuntarily, 'Does it come up to expectations?'

'The dress? Over and beyond with you in it, Miss Lindwall.'

Her lips twitched. 'You look rather nice yourself, Mr Jones.' He wore cream gaberdine, well-pressed trousers and a taupe, round-necked knitted sports shirt.

'*Thank* you.' He raised an amused eyebrow at her then laughed and reached for her hand. 'Dominique, that's the nicest thing you've ever said to me—I'm glad we're not fighting any longer.'

'Yes, well...' She frowned, but there was a humorous glint in her green eyes. 'I don't quite know how you achieved it but so am I.'

The restaurant was on a first-floor covered veranda, with candles on the tables and a view over Hastings Street, and the food was delicious.

And something happened to Dominique as they ate slowly, talking casually and companionably, laughing sometimes at the things he said, and shared a bottle of wine—well, it had been happening ever since she'd woken up from her sleep, she realised. A gradual lessening of the tension in her and a growing pleasure in his company, which was rather incredible considering the gesture he'd made only that morning.

She thought, ruefully, of the young sales assistant whom he'd completely bowled over and her words...'*he's so nice, as well as—*'

'Something's amusing you, Dominique?'

She came out of her reverie and glanced at him wryly. 'Yes. You.' She sipped her wine.

He looked at her quizzically. 'That wasn't *quite* the effect I was trying to achieve.'

'Weren't you?' She gazed at him with something at the back of her mind that refused to make itself clear, then shrugged lightly. 'You shouldn't worry about it; I was only thinking how nice you can be at times—how quite fatally nice.'

Their gazes locked suddenly. He said slowly, 'I'm not sure if that's a compliment.'

She stirred and looked away. 'I meant it as one, all the same.'

'It doesn't make me feel as if you view me—as if you feel there's much *depth* to me, however,'

'Oh, I'm sure there is. Too much, perhaps.'

'Why don't you explain, Dominique?' he said after a moment.

'No, I don't think I should,' she said quietly, looking down at her glass, then up into his eyes suddenly. 'That was a lovely meal. Thank you. I'm ready to go whenever you are.'

He narrowed his eyes slightly. 'Shall we take a short stroll? To work off our meal?'

'If you like…'

So that was what they did—strolled down Hastings Street then came back via the beach with their shoes in their hands.

'We seem to make a habit of this,' she said as she rinsed her feet beneath the hotel tap.

'Yes.'

'And this?' she said a little unevenly a few minutes later inside their suite as they stood facing each other.

He hadn't put the main lights on and he'd made no attempt to touch her, but there was now a doubt in her mind about what was to come, because his mood was different, she sensed. The laughter seemed to have gone, and in its place was an electric tension between them that was almost tangible—yet it was *he* who had wanted laughter…

'Yes, and this,' he murmured. 'If you want it, Dominique.'

'Yes,' she said, and stood quite still as everything came together for her in a sudden flash of clarity.

She'd denied earlier that she was capable of a light-hearted, no-regrets approach to sleeping with him yet she couldn't deny to herself or him any longer that it was what she wanted to do—rather overwhelmingly, in fact. But the problem of where it would lead still remained, and she saw suddenly that she had no idea.

So why are you doing it? she asked herself, and suddenly remembered that cool, pitying look in Anna Graham's eyes. Which led her to remember why *he* might be doing it, and to understand that keeping it fairly light might be his way of protecting her, despite his denial that he wanted to keep it light-hearted earlier.

Was she being foolish not to offer *herself* this form of protection if she was going to do it? Protection against a man who might never be for her but who might be able to exorcise some ghosts, the aura of having been left at the altar...? But was he now unsure that she would be able to play the game his way? She swallowed suddenly and said, 'Would you excuse me for a moment?'

He frowned, then nodded and turned away.

What she did took her about ten minutes and she did it all in the privacy of the bathroom. She took off the pearl-coloured silk dress and cleansed her face. She let out her hair and brushed it, as well as brushing her teeth. Then she removed her underwear and slipped into his ivory satin nightgown that came down to her ankles. As a final touch she sprayed some Poison onto her wrists.

She looked at herself steadily in the mirror for a moment, then turned away, put the light out and walked back into the lounge.

He was standing with his back to her, looking out over the terrace, and the room was quiet and still dimly lit, with the only sound of the rhythmic crash of the surf on the beach. Nor did she make a sound, but he turned after a moment and narrowed his eyes again as his blue gaze drifted over her, taking in the curly mass of her hair slipped behind her ears, the slim gown with its narrow straps and V of lace down the front, her bare feet, then came back to her eyes.

And he spoke at last, very quietly. 'You're beautiful, Dominique. Come here.' He held out his hand.

She walked slowly towards him, searching his eyes, conscious again of how the laughter had gone, how the niceness of the afternoon, which had relaxed her and made him fun to be with, had also gone, and she stopped just out of his reach and said huskily, all her logic suddenly at sixes and sevens, 'Something's gone wrong, hasn't it?'

'No. Not if you're sure you want to do this.'

'It's a bit late to ask me that.'

They stared into each other's eyes, and his were curiously sombre as he said nothing.

'I thought this—' she smoothed the satin of the nightgown then looked into his eyes '—might show that I'm no longer adopting a do-or-die attitude. I thought you might appreciate that.'

'I might—' he lifted his shoulders a little restlessly '—if I understood what was behind it.'

'Nothing,' she said, and hoped that the effort she was making wasn't obvious, because she was suddenly determined to go on as she had planned, and had been made so, she realised, through a totally *irrational* desire to show Rory Jones that as he'd made all the running after that first night he couldn't back out now because he'd become afraid that she mightn't play the game the way he wanted. 'I also wore this...' she began quietly. 'Well, I'm not very practised at...at seduction and I guess it shows. Sorry.' And she turned away.

She heard his breath expel and felt his hand on her arm, and he swung her, not gently, back to face him. 'Dominique, you seduced me that first night,' he said roughly. 'Without even trying. But you can't deny it's been—heavy work ever since then.'

'I'm not,' she whispered. 'Which is why I find this—your sudden reluctance when I've come about—a bit of a surprise.'

'As does your—about-face come as a bit of a surprise, I guess. I just wish I knew what was going on behind those beautiful green eyes, that's all.' His fingers about her arm were hard.

'Well, I'm relieved there's *something* you don't understand about me. It proves if nothing else that I'm not quite so transparent or easily dissected, and that you're not as good with women as you think.' And a glint of anger lit those green eyes as she stared defiantly up at him.

He swore. 'Do you really believe I think that?'

'I'm waiting to find out,' she flung back at him.

His fingers tightened on her, then he jerked her into his arms, saying between his teeth, 'OK—here goes!'

'Rory...?'

He stirred beside her. 'Dominique?'

She closed her eyes. Her beautiful nightgown had been discarded on the floor beside the bed together with his clothes, and their lovemaking had been wild, passionate, bruising and the most stunning, exciting thing that had ever happened to her. She'd arched her body against his, wound her legs around him, offered him her breasts but withheld her mouth, held him in her arms yet tantalised him, then accepted the sweet torture as he too had tantalised all the secret, sensitive places of her body. 'You were right. The answer to every maiden's prayer, in fact,' she whispered.

'Oh, hell,' he said softly, and gathered her so that her head rested on his shoulder and her body curved against his and then pulled the sheet up. 'No, it wasn't that.'

'It wasn't? You could have fooled me. I may have been completely inexperienced, but there are some things you just know—' She stopped abruptly. 'I hope I wasn't *too* inexperienced,' she said rather shakenly.

'Dominique, I meant—it was us; we couldn't have done it without each other. You were sensational.'

'But I started out so angry with you.' She bit her lip then laughed. 'And look at me now.'

'I would love to.' He pushed himself up on one elbow and swept the sheet aside.

'No, I didn't mean—'

'I know you didn't, but all the same it's a delight I can't deny myself.' And he drew his hand gently down her body. 'Such a work of art,' he murmured, and smiled into her eyes. 'And if, as you once said to me, you thought being an accountant made for a lack of poetry in your soul, you made love to me with all sorts of fire and poetry and grace.'

'I sometimes wondered if I was destined to stay a virgin,' she said involuntarily, and bit her lip.

He smoothed her hair, kissed her lightly, then lay down again and cradled her in his arms. He said simply, 'Tell me one thing—are you happy you didn't?'

She thought for a bit, with a touch of colour staining her cheeks, then said huskily, 'Yes. What do we do now?'

'We could sleep,' he suggested.

'I mean… No, you're right.' And she yawned, moved her cheek on his shoulder and felt her eyelids grow heavy.

The next thing she was conscious of was the delicious aroma of frying bacon.

Dominique opened her eyes, stretched, sniffed then frowned, and realised that she was alone in the bed and it *was* bacon she could smell, and that she was starving. She got up and put on the white towelling robe that came with the suite and walked into the main room, to be amazed at the sight of Rory Jones in blue shorts and a blue and white striped T-shirt cooking breakfast.

'Good morning. This is a surprise!'

He turned and grinned at her. 'I thought it might be easier than going out for breakfast.'

'But…how…?'

'I popped down the road and got a few supplies—bread, butter, eggs, bacon and some juice and some fruit.'

'Very commendable,' she commented with a glint of laughter in her eyes. 'But why easier?'

'Ah.' He put down the spatula he was wielding. 'I'll show you.' He crossed the room to her and stood looking down at her, a little glint in his own eyes. 'Good morning, Dominique—may I?'

But he didn't wait for permission. He took her in his arms and kissed her deeply, then he pushed the robe off her shoulders and kissed her neck, her shoulders, her breasts until she said unsteadily, 'I get the picture.' And she ran her fingers through his hair.

He lifted his head and grinned wickedly down into her eyes. 'It's also about to pour.'

'Oh!' She moved in his arms and glanced outside. 'I hadn't noticed.'

He laughed and hugged her. 'Which means once we've had our breakfast and—assuaged any other types of hunger that might strike us, we could, instead of having a swim, try out that large spa-bath at our leisure. So, you see, it's much more practical to have breakfast at home, in a manner of speaking, under these circumstances.'

'I have to agree—it would be a pity if it got burnt, though,' she murmured gravely.

'Hell!' He kissed her lightly and let her go. 'I must have been getting carried away—I wonder why?'

'This is heavenly!' she said dreamily some time later as she lay in his arms with her back to him in the steamy, bubbled-filled spa-bath and he soaped her body.

'Haven't you ever done this before?'

'Yes, but rather obviously, I should have thought, not with a man,' she teased.

'You should always do it with a man,' he said seriously. 'There's really no other way.'

She laughed softly. 'Any man?'

'No, definitely not.' He soaped her breasts and trickled water over them. 'A man of discernment and refinement is absolutely essential for this kind of thing, and—'

'Such as yourself?'

'Well, I do try to give utmost satisfaction,' he said. 'And—'

'You're being modest again, Rory!' she quipped.

'I rather think you trapped me into this one,' he replied wryly.

'No, I didn't,' she denied. 'You were the one who enlarged upon the beneficial qualities of doing it with a man—'

'Ah, but was I wrong?' he countered.

She slipped out of his grasp and turned over to face him so that she was lying on his chest, and looked up at him as he leant back against the edge of the bath, his hair sleek and wet, his blue eyes quizzically amused. 'In your usual highly *immodest* way,' she teased, 'you were very right, Mr Emory Jones.'

'And you, Miss Lindwall—' he ran his hands over her body beneath the surface of the water '—remind me of a highly desirable mermaid, quite capable of luring men to all sorts of things.'

'Not this morning. I mean not to anything disastrous this morning; I'm in too good a mood.' She propped her chin on her fists on his chest and added softly, 'Thanks to you.'

'You have a strange way of apportioning the credit—for an accountant, too!' It was his turn to tease.

'No, I haven't.' She sobered suddenly. 'Whatever happens I'll never regret this, because in one night you've done more for me than I thought possible. I also feel a little foolish,' she confessed, 'to think of the fight I put up and the fuss I made.'

'Dominique—don't,' he said quietly, and fiddled with the wet strands of her hair. 'It mightn't have been so momentous if you hadn't.'

She grimaced. 'That's a concept that is going to take—' She stopped as the phone rang.

He groaned. 'Bloody hell!'

'You'd better answer it.' She moved away so that he could reach the phone beside the bath, then when it turned out to be his secretary with all sorts of messages she kissed him on the nose, climbed out and waved impishly to him.

'Dominique, hang on—hell!' he said, and added to his secretary, 'No, not you, I've been abandoned in the bath... No, by a mermaid... Maureen, can I ring you back in about five minutes?' He put the phone down.

Dominique stopped in the act of wrapping herself in a large towel and raised an eyebrow at him. 'I hope you haven't shocked your Maureen rigid.'

'She's past being shocked by me,' he replied, and deftly removed the towel.

'What are you doing?'

'Well, *I'm* not past being—devastated by the untimely removal of your presence. That's all,' he said, and held her against him. 'Especially all satiny and slippery and wet,' he said softly, and moulded her hips to his.

'Or do you think you simply have to have the last word?'

He removed his hands from her hips and folded her in his arms. 'That too, perhaps.'

'I knew it!'

'Yes, well,' he said wryly, 'we're coming to know each other a lot better, aren't we, Dominique?' And he kissed her. Then he released her and said, 'Tell you what, why don't we get a video? It's pouring now.'

'It's only ten o'clock in the morning,' Dominique protested.

'How decadent!' he mocked gently.

'Well, all right, let's be decadent,' she said ruefully.

and get it while you ring poor Maureen

around his waist... ...he towel.

...uests?' ...tied his towel

tive.' ...ior mo-

'What's that?'

He wrapped her in her towel sarong-wise, took her hand and led her to the lounge. 'See this exceedingly comfortable settee placed exceedingly strategically for television viewing?'

'I do.'

'See how excessively hard it's raining?' He gestured to the terrace, where indeed the rain was pelting down so heavily that the view beyond was totally obscured.

'Yes.'

'Well, what better way to watch a movie than lying together, warm and dry—and very close?'

'At ten o'clock in the morning,' Dominique said gravely.

'At ten in the morning,' he agreed, and raised an amused eyebrow at her. 'Is that something else you've never done?'

She touched his face lightly with her fingertips. 'Yes. It sounds very pleasant, however.'

He caught her hand, folded it and kissed her knuckles. 'I'll try my best to make it so, Dominique!'

'I believe you,' she laughed. 'We could even devise a name for this exercise, couldn't we?'

He eyed her quizzically. 'Such as?'

'The...Liberalisation of Dominique Lindwall?' she suggested.

His eyes softened. 'We ... PLAYBOY LO... ... worried
phone rang again. ...ermaid, possibly.'
'Ah, Maureen ... ...ue,' he replied, and picked up
that you've b...
'Oh, I...
the ...

She chose a *Lethal Weapon* movie from the library at
Reception, as well as a couple of classical CDs. It was
her choice of movie that prompted Rory to say, 'You
surprise me. I didn't think this would be your kind of
thing.'

'No? What did you think would be my kind of
thing?' She was lying in his arms on the settee as he'd
predicted, and they'd drawn the wooden louvres against
the storm and switched on a lamp.

He moved his chin on her hair. 'Something more cultured.'

She smiled. 'You mean you took me for a bit of a
culture snob—I wonder why?'

'Perhaps it's to do with being such a serious, sober
accountant normally. It seems I was wrong.'

'Well, no,' she confessed. 'I don't normally go for
this kind of thing.'

'Then why?'

'It struck me,' she said gravely, 'that I've always fan-
cied Mel Gibson.'

'I'm undone!'

'No, you're not,' she denied. 'Anyway, it also struck
me that I've been too sober and serious for too long; I
may have mentioned it earlier, but anyway, hush—I
need to concentrate.'

He laughed and kissed her. 'Anything you say,
ma'am.'

So they watched Mel Gibson and Danny Glover, chuckling together at times, and Dominique found herself thoroughly entertained. At the end Rory said to her, 'So what's your verdict about the decadent practice of watching movies in the morning?'

'I'm impressed,' she replied, stretching then settling back in his arms. 'It's still raining.'

'So it is. Should we order some lunch from Room Service, or brave the weather?'

She turned her head to look into his eyes. 'Let's stay here.'

'Done!'

They lunched on oysters and open roast-beef sandwiches, then, mysteriously, she felt sleepy, and did sleep for a couple of hours.

'I don't know what's wrong with me,' she said fretfully when she got up to find him reading peacefully in the lounge.

He shot her a laughing look.

'Well, perhaps I do,' she conceded, and sat down beside him to rub her face and run her hands through her hair. The phone rang. He got up to answer it, then put it down thoughtfully. She raised her eyebrows at him.

'A request for you to get in touch with Frank Conrod.'

'Why?' Her eyes widened.

'I don't know, but you don't have to; for all he knows, you're not contactable at the moment. Maureen is very discreet.'

Her lips parted. 'Do you mean you told her to be?'

He shrugged. 'Yes.'

'But it—' Dominique gestured '—could be something urgent connected with another of my clients—I think I ought to, just in case…'

He smiled slightly. 'What if he asks you where you are?'

Dominique hesitated. 'Perhaps you're right.'

'On the other hand—' he studied her critically '—if it's going to *worry* you, you could always be mysteriously evasive. I am paying for your time, so it's up to me how you spend it.'

'Rory,' she said slowly, paling a little. 'I—'

But he grimaced and took her hand and pulled her up. 'Only joking. Ring him, Dominique. I can see it's going to niggle away at you if you don't.'

'Mr Conrod, it's Dominique Lindwall… Yes, I'm fine, thank you… Yes, it's going well; I'm—acquiring a more comprehensive view of the Jones empire… No, I'm not actually at Mount Livingstone at the moment, but I've seen it. Is there a problem? No? I see. Well, thank you for your call, but I do have everything under control at this end and I should be back on schedule by the end of the week. Yes… Thank you again… Goodbye.'

She put down the phone ruefully and turned to Rory, who said softly and wickedly, 'Do you have everything under control at this end, Dominique?'

She blushed, started to disclaim, then buried her head against his shoulder. 'Don't make fun of me, Rory. I feel enough of a fool as it is.'

He looked wryly down at the top of her head, then stroked her hair. 'Frank was only fishing?'

'Yes…'

'I wonder why?'

'I...' She bit her lip. 'I made a bit of a fuss about doing this.'

'I thought you might have.'

'Well... But things have changed, and you can't accuse me of, well—adjusting to the change *ungraciously*, can you?'

He took her chin in his fingers and tilted it so that he could look into he eyes—a long, surprisingly sober look, that made her heart start to beat a little faster for some reason—until he said, still soberly, 'No, I can't accuse you of anything like that, Dominique.'

'Rory, I...perhaps we should talk about—'

'No,' he interrupted, and kissed her lightly. 'I've got a better idea. Have you any kind of a waterproof jacket with you?'

'Yes, just a light one, but—'

'Good. Let's go for a long, long walk.'

She blinked a bit dazedly. 'It's still raining.'

'It's actually settled to a fine, steady drizzle, and it's certainly not cold. How about it? Or is walking in the rain something else you've never done?'

'No,' she said slowly. 'I'm not that repressed.'

'I didn't say you were, but why the reluctance?'

She blinked once more, then her mouth curved softly. 'You're on, Mr Jones. I suppose this is "real" walking again?'

'You're dead right, Miss Lindwall!'

CHAPTER EIGHT

THEY got back an hour and a half later, breathless, soaking and exhilarated. They'd walked up the hill, through the national park, back down again and along the beach to the mouth of the river.

They looked at each other as they dripped onto the tiled floor, laughed and said together, 'A spa!'

'Great minds think alike, Dominique,' Rory drawled.

'Oh, I don't know,' she answered. 'Without a bath, if I were to sit down I might never get up again. Your "real" walking is a true test of one's muscles.'

So they soaked amidst the bubbling, reviving jets of the spa-bath until she said that she felt restored.

'Good,' he said, and kissed her. 'But there's no hurry. I'll get us a drink while you finish off.'

She lay alone in the bath for about ten minutes longer, then got out, dried herself, slipped on the white towelling robe and combed and dried the excess moisture out of her hair.

Rory was waiting for her in the lounge, clad similarly, lying back on the settee with his feet up on the low table and a bottle of French champagne in a frosted silver bucket reposing beside two tall glasses. One of the CDs she'd chosen was playing softly and there was only one lamp on.

'Cheers,' he said quietly, sitting up and pouring the champagne.

'Cheers. Thank you.' She accepted her glass and wandered over to the glass doors with it, but it was pitch-dark outside now and the rain was still thrumming down onto the terrace. She grimaced. 'We certainly brought the rain.'

'Does it matter?'

She turned and discovered that he was standing behind her. 'No. It's rather nice. I feel...' she paused '...insulated in our own little world. But if you're such an energetic person as everyone claims and as you do, from time to time, demonstrate—how will it affect you?'

'Right at this moment—' he looked down at her '—I'm very agreeably affected.'

'Ah...' Dominique took a little breath and drank half a glass of champagne as her pulses started to beat heavily.

'So how does that affect you, Dominique?' he said very quietly.

'It...' she looked down at her glass then answered honestly '...excites me...'

He took her glass from her, surprised her by picking her up and sitting her on the room divider then offering her her glass back. 'Tell me more,' he invited with his lips twisting and a lazy glint in his eyes that she just knew was wildly deceptive.

'Well—' she sipped some more champagne '—it's a bit difficult to put into words, but I suppose I'm wondering if what happened last night can happen the same way again, or whether it was one of those one-off experiences—'

'Not a chance,' he murmured. 'Not the way I'm feeling right now.'

She smiled faintly. 'But I'm not burning with righteous indignation this time,' she reminded him.

'Well, I *am* burning with—something.' And he undid the sash of her robe.

'Rory,' she said on an indrawn breath.

'Dominique?'

'Nothing…' She looked down as the robe parted, exposing her breasts, and then into his eyes.

'Comfortable, then?'

'I…yes, but—'

He put his glass down, took hers from her and put it down too and slid his hands around her waist beneath the robe, and it slipped off her shoulders.

'Lovely, crushed rose velvet nipples and pale, full breasts that have tormented me since that first night. I kept thinking of them in the most unlikely places, thinking of how they would feel in my hands.' He cupped them. 'Firm, ripe…and how they would taste,' he said barely audibly.

'Rory.' She closed her eyes and tilted her head back as he did just that—tasted each nipple then bit them gently in turn. 'Oh, God,' she whispered as she was racked with desire, and slid her hands into his hair.

But he hadn't finished the sweet torment, it seemed. He raised his head at last, smiled into her dazed eyes and removed her robe further so that she was sitting on it, surrounded by it but naked from the waist up in the lamplight. And he drew his hands down her back, down her arms, down her sides, across her waist, and she closed her eyes again and stretched her throat back, succumbing to the sheer pleasure of it.

'What are you doing to me?' she said huskily at last, resting her brow on his and linking her hands behind his neck.

'Don't you like it?'

'I'm…dying slowly from it.'

'So am I,' he said wryly. 'You could—take me, Dominique.'

She lifted her head and looked into his eyes. 'Here?'

'Here and now,' he responded. 'But you might need to take this off first.'

'Oh…' Her lips parted but she undid his robe and it fell to the floor, and she succumbed for a while to another pleasure—that of being able to run her own hands over his shoulders and back.

Until he said softly, 'Put your legs around me.' She did, and was strangely affected by the golden gleam of her skin against the darker tan of his, by the intermingling of their limbs in a position that she would never have dreamt of adopting but one that filled her with a wild sort of freedom and a growing need to give and receive. Then he said with an interrogative little glint in his eyes, 'Now?'

'Yes, please, now,' she gasped. And he cupped her hips and thrust into her, causing her to cry out softly with pleasure, and to climax immediately with his head crushed to her breasts.

'I told you,' he said some time later, when they were wrapped in each other's arms but lying on the settee now and modestly clad in their robes again. 'Here, have some more champagne,' he added gently, and moved so that she could sit up enough to drink.

'Do I look as if I need it?' she said ruefully, but sipped it gratefully.

'You look wonderful.' He stared down for a moment at her mass of hair, the still-dazed green of her eyes. 'But a little shocked,' he said wryly, and kissed her forehead lightly.

'Another step towards the Liberalisation of Dominique Lindwall,' she murmured.

He paused, then said with a faint frown in his eyes, 'Did you mind?'

'Mind?' She laughed softly, but with a certain amount of self-directed mockery. 'I'd be hard put to it to make that stick, wouldn't I?'

'Well—do you mind *not* being able to mind, then?'

'Rory—no, how could I?' she said with a faint tinge of colour coming into her cheeks. 'That would make me— I'd rather not think about it,' she added confusedly.

'Good,' he drawled, with a wicked little glint in his eyes. 'Now for the next big question—you may or may not have noticed, but it's time to eat again. Should we dine in or out?'

Her mouth curved. 'How come you're not fat—the opposite, if anything?' she queried.

'I burn up a lot of energy,' he replied seriously. 'Does that mean you're not hungry?'

She considered and discovered that she was. 'Well, yes, I am, now you come to mention it. I just hadn't had time to think about it.'

'There is a small, unpretentious place I know of that happens to serve wonderful meals—it's not far away but we could drive so we wouldn't get wet again, and you could almost come as you are.'

She laughed up at him. 'Surely not?'

'Well, with a few modifications—a quick shower, a pair of jeans and a shirt, that's all. Would you be happy to do that?'

'Entirely happy,' she said, with a contented little smile this time. 'Would you?'

'Lady,' he said, 'I'm all yours to command at the moment.'

His restaurant was little more than a pavement café protected from the weather with roll-down clear plastic blinds. It had plain scrubbed deal tables, thick white china, old lanterns and a potted hedge separating it from pedestrians, but the food was marvellous.

'Being with you is also a culinary delight,' Dominique said as she sat back with a sigh to enjoy her coffee after a meal of delicious *escargots*, home-baked bread and golden grilled fillets of fresh, caught-that-day sea perch.

'Was it not so with Bryce?'

She looked up quickly in surprise, but his eyes were steady and very blue. She took a breath. 'He was very much into fine dining,' she said slowly, 'but not the kind that actually appealed to me greatly. I mean to say that I came to think that the ambience of the restaurant and—' she gestured wryly '—how much it cost meant more to him than the fact they served artistic meals that didn't seem to have much taste.'

'Ah, *nouvelle cuisine*.'

'You don't approve either?' She thought of the meals that had been served at Mount Livingstone—wonderful roast lamb one night, a steak and kidney stew swimming with little, light-as-air dumplings another night.

'They always leave me ravenous and irritable, those kinds of meals. I prefer my art on the walls and my food ungarnished by spikes of this, rosettes and strange leaves of that.'

Dominique smiled across the table at him, her eyes warm and a little wondering. She'd left her hair loose and it was curling wildly at her shoulders, and he put out a hand and touched it, then covered her hand as it lay on the tables. 'You're a sight for sore eyes, you know.'

'Thank you,' she whispered.

He picked up her hand and linked his fingers through hers, their elbows resting on the table. 'No, don't thank me, Dominique; you're rather unique, and don't let anyone ever tell you differently. Unfortunately,' he said before she could speak, 'I'm going to have to take you back to Netanya and take you straight to bed.'

She caught her breath, her eyes widening.

'Yes,' he said ruefully. 'The way you look and the memory of certain events between us have caused certain other events, and it's steadily growing more urgent.'

'Oh...' She went pink, but her eyes laughed at him. 'I don't know if I'm up to another session on the room divider,' she teased.

He grinned back but said wickedly, 'All I need this time is a bed, that's all.'

Yet despite his protestations or urgency it was sweet, simple love that they made this time, but it filled her with an amazing warmth. And they fell asleep in each other's arms.

They also woke to a minor miracle—bright sunshine and a clear sky. They looked at each other and said together, 'A swim!'

This time she wore her new white bikini, and he took one look at her and whistled expressively. 'Was I ever right about that!'

'Now, don't get too full of yourself, Mr Jones,' she

advised, then relented, 'This is another first, incidentally.'

'Never worn a bikini before?' He raised an eyebrow.

'Not since I was about twelve—I know, I know—I—'

'No, you don't, Miss Lindwall.' He caught her about the waist. 'You have no idea what I was going to say, at least.'

'What?' she asked softly.

'That I'm glad—and particularly glad that I'm the first to see you looking so stunning in one that I chose with my own hand.'

'You are nice, you know,' she said, 'despite your incurable modesty.'

'And you're so nice we'd better get out of here before I'm tempted to take you back to bed.'

'Oh, definitely,' she teased.

They swam, jogged up the beach and swam again, and the clear, beautiful, new-washed day and sparkling surf had nearly the same effect as drinking champagne, Dominique thought as they finally walked back to the suite.

'I feel quite heady with delight,' she said to him. 'I feel like a new person. If you were to— No, if you were to let me cook *you* bacon and eggs this morning... Are there any left?'

'There are.'

'I would like to do that, then.'

'With pleasure.' And in plain sight of everyone who happened to be about he took her into his arms and kissed her leisurely. 'Now that,' he murmured, 'makes *me* quite heady with delight.'

But back in their suite the message light on the phone

was blinking frenziedly and he grimaced, but showered first before he sat down at the desk and picked it up.

Dominique showered herself, and put her shorts and yellow T-shirt on, then pottered about happily making breakfast while he had a fairly long conversation with the faceless Maureen and made a few more calls.

So taken up was she with her preparations that she didn't tune in to what he was saying at all, and it came as some surprise when he put the phone down for the last time, swivelled the chair round and said, 'Dominique—come here.'

She went, but with a faint frown in her eyes at the different note in his voice. 'What is it?'

'Sit down,' he murmured, and drew her down onto his knee. 'I have to go back to Brisbane this morning. Something's come up.'

There was a little pause, then she said, 'Business?'

'Yes—plus a problem at Mount Livingstone.'

'What?' Her eyes widened.

'Anna and Bernard have gone back to Waverley Downs, and without Luke—plus the fact that the place is all but cut off by flood waters now and only accessible by air—I need to be there after I've done what I have to do in Brisbane.'

'Of course,' Dominique said slowly. 'So—' her voice shook '—our little holiday has to end? No,' she added as he cupped her cheek, 'I mean…it's just taken me by surprise, that's all. Of course it had to end.'

'That's not to say this will be the end of us, though.'

'Rory—' she closed her eyes briefly '—what is to become of us? I've started to ask this before, but you've cut me off each time—even last night you said something that made me wonder. And I know I'm probably…jumping the gun, but could you at least tell me one thing?'

'What?' He stared into her eyes narrowly.

'Is Anna Graham…in your blood in a way no other woman could be?'

'Dominique,' he said after an age, and his eyes were curiously bleak. 'No. I neither trust nor even like her these days, and I wouldn't want her if I could have her, but—there still remains the problem of whether I'm the right man for a girl like you.'

'Oh, God,' she whispered. 'I thought—I wondered all along if this was…just an exercise in rehabilitation. Perhaps you shouldn't have done it so well—but that's what you do, don't you?' She licked some tears off her lip, not caring that she was crying.

'What do I do?'

'Rehabilitate women then send them off—'

'Dominique,' he said harshly, 'no, I don't. And it never was that.'

'Then what?' she whispered.

'A far stronger compulsion than I've known for years,' he said evenly. 'But while I can't tell you that I know where it will lead I can tell you this—I'm a loner and a wanderer, Dominique. I'm the kind of man who would be hell to live with, and much as I would love to change myself for you…and I've said that to no one…it would only be dishonest to let you think I could.'

Dominique took a distraught breath and her gaze fell on the room divider behind her. 'You should have told me this before…last night.'

'Should I?' he said very quietly. 'I didn't think any-thing could flaw that for us.'

Dominique sat in disbelieving, agonised silence, then

she said vaguely, 'Oh, the bacon! I turned it off but it'll be getting soggy—or something. Like me!' She laughed, but it came out as a hiccup, and she stood up, trying to evade his hands until he let her go.

'Dominique—what if I suggested you came with me?'

'I...' She turned to stare down at him. 'For how long?' she whispered.

'For as long as we both wanted it.'

'You mean—to be your mistress?' Their eyes clashed until she looked away abruptly and went over to the kitchenette where, instead of the bacon, she suddenly saw herself in her apartment, staring at the phone, and saw her father's face... 'No.' She took a sobbing little breath. 'I couldn't. I—just couldn't.'

'Do you think I don't know that? Do you think I'd *like* to see you tearing yourself apart, battling your in-bred morals?' His gaze held hers steadily.

She stared back into his eyes and understood suddenly. 'Is that why you're not asking me to?'

'Would you rather I'd told you this at some later date?'

She closed her eyes and turned away.

'Dominique,' he said quietly, 'look at me.'

'No, Rory, I can't.' In truth she couldn't see much at all through the sudden veil of tears.

'You said nothing could make you regret certain things,' he reminded her in that same quiet, controlled voice.

She grimaced and wiped her eyes on the back of her hand. 'Famous last words—do they all give this much trouble when it comes to the parting of the ways? Does it always come so *soon*?'

'Look, for one thing there've not been nearly as many as you imagine.'

'How many, then?' She tried to sound flippant but it didn't come off, although she persisted, 'Ten? Twenty?'

'No, nothing like that,' he said evenly. 'I—' He stopped. 'I tend to avoid it wherever possible if I can. This playboy image you've accused me of is actually something else.'

'*What?*' Dominique turned to look at him at last.

He smiled unamusedly. 'It's a bit of a cover—there's safety in numbers.' And for a moment there was something incredibly bleak in his eyes.

But what happened to Dominique was quite different. It was as if the scales fell from her eyes and she suddenly saw the real Rory Jones—a man who was too good with women for his own good, a man who recognised this, didn't take much pleasure in it and lived the rest of his life at a pace to compensate for it. A man who had only once found the love he'd sought and had then had it denied to him but was not prepared to compromise...

But why me? she wondered, and the last piece of the puzzle clicked into place.

'I should have known,' she whispered, her eyes suddenly stricken.

'Known what?'

'I should have known when you still wanted to keep it light. I should have known when there was that odd reluctance—even last night when you talked about Bryce... It was the fight I put up, wasn't it?'

'Not in the first place, no,' he said grimly. 'I did take one look at you and—'

'But even then,' she broke in, 'you thought I looked bored and proud. Do you know, I think I would have been much better off now, Rory Jones, if I'd keeled over that first night, as all the other want to do? Because then you would have found some charming, *light-hearted* way of walking away and that would have been that.'

'Dominique,' he said a little roughly, '*would* you rather I'd let it go on for months and then told you this?'

'No, I would rather like to think that what's happened between us over these last couple of days has given you grounds to…hope. Or, if not, then I'd much rather you'd *listened* to me and left me alone.'

'Left you the way you were?' he said barely audibly. 'With a wedding dress still hanging in the closet of your mind like a skeleton,' he said deliberately. 'With no knowledge that there's more to life than accountability, rationality and assessment, and one—no, make that two men's assessments of *you* that were entirely selfish and quite wrong, as it happens—your father's and Bryce Denver's. With no knowledge that you had far more to give than they ever deserved. More passion, more sheer life in you than they ever even took the time to suspect.'

'And no one to give it to.'

'That will change one day.'

Dominique closed her eyes. 'That was something else you said last night. In a roundabout kind of way… "You're rather unique, and don't let anyone ever tell you differently…" But not quite unique enough for you. Wouldn't it be funny if I went away with a new set of complexes?'

'Look,' he said abruptly, 'it's not a question of you not being good enough for me; it's the other way around.'

She turned away convulsively and looked at the bacon with despair. 'Sorry, I don't feel like breakfast now.

I...yes, you may have shown me that there's more to me, and you're probably right—some fundamentals about me *will* never change.' She shrugged and wiped her nose on the back of her hand. 'But you can't expect me to admire— Did you never stop to think that I might fall in love with you along this road to liberalising me?'

He was silent for a long time, then he said, 'It might feel that way now, but somewhere out there is the right man for you—a much better man for you than I could ever be. What will you do?' he added.

'Do? Now?' She grimaced. 'Go back to Conrod, Whitney & Smith. Oh, hell...' She blinked back a fresh set of tears. 'Look—why don't you set up that holding company with your own accountant? It's really the best advice I can give you professionally. And even Frank Conrod would have to agree. Particularly if we didn't lose our external audit of all your companies.'

'I would never do that to you, Dominique.'

She smiled faintly. 'And I do have enough to work on now for us not to have to deal directly in the meantime.'

He captured her gaze and held it, and at last she found the composure for it not to waver. 'Dominique, will you do one thing for me?'

'What?'

'Never take second best again—from me or anyone else.'

'I'll...' She swallowed. 'I'll try. If you would do one thing for me?'

He gazed at her sombrely.

'There must be someone out there for *you* to love as you once wanted to all those years ago—don't stop looking.'

He closed his eyes and a nerve twitched in his jawline. Then he put a hand on her hair and took it away almost immediately; he smiled perfunctorily. 'I'll try...'

'Messages, messages, messages—where do I begin?' Sally was perched on the corner of Dominique's desk in her usual spot. 'Let's see—Gayle Gyngell almost every day. And...' She reeled off a string of names, mostly clients. 'Plus—now, this one I'm in two minds over, but he has rung twice.' She stopped and placed her pad face-down in her lap. 'Dominique, I really don't know whether to be a good secretary or a good friend.'

'Sally,' Dominique said with a sigh, 'much as I appreciate your sentiments, I haven't got time for semantics. Who has rung twice?'

'Your ex,' Sally said slowly.

'Oh!'

'Uh-huh.'

'What did you tell him?'

'That you were out of town, that's all. It's not my place to give people your every movement,' Sally said virtuously, then grimaced.

'So?' Dominique eyed her.

'Well, I did tell one person, but really she wormed it out of me in a highly unethical way.'

Dominique groaned. 'Not Gayle?'

'Yes—Miss Gyngell; sorry,' Sally said contritely. 'But you would have to be a slab of concrete to resist her.'

'That means it will be all over town,' Dominique said cynically.

'She did swear she wouldn't tell a soul—'

'Anything can happen with Gayle in the heat of the moment,' Dominique mused, recalling how Belinda Miller had made the connection. 'Oh, well—'

'Not,' Sally interrupted with a little frown, 'that there's any particular reason for people not to know—or is there?'

'No,' Dominique said briefly.

'So how did it go? You got a bit of sun, by the look of it.'

'There's plenty of sun out there,' Dominique agreed.

'On the other hand you look a bit tired. Was he a right handful? Emory Jones?'

'You could say that.'

'Well, you certainly said it with some irony.'

'Sally—' Dominique looked at her both wearily and warily '—would you mind leaving me to return all these calls?'

'OK—are you going to call *him* back?'

'Bryce?'

'Yes.'

'No.'

'Well, that's one good thing!' Sally said brightly, and departed.

But Dominique didn't lift her phone immediately. She sat back instead, and rubbed the back of her neck, and wished that she could blank out her mind to everything but work. But it was only yesterday that she'd flown to Brisbane, in a strained silence for the most part, from the Sunshine Coast and, from there, travelled down to the Gold Coast in a private hire car, alone.

Fortunately the flight had been very brief, and Rory had arranged to have the car waiting beside the tarmac at Archerfield Airfield. But, brief as their parting formalities had been, all told, they'd represented an enormous strain on her in a variety of ways—disbelief, anger and then, like a knife to her heart, the incredibly poignant sensation of seeing him standing beside the plane, in his bomber jacket, brown moleskins and hiking boots, raising his hand in final farewell as she was driven away.

And that evening, alone in her apartment, as she'd tried to take stock and piece it all together—tried to piece *herself* together, had come the doubts that she'd done the right thing. Doubts as to whether she should have dismissed her morals and her repressions and insisted that she was capable of staying with Rory Jones under any circumstances and whether she would be haunted for the rest of her life by a sarong, a bikini, a silk dress and a satin nightgown in her closet.

Work, she now thought dully; that's the only solution, and she put her hand on the phone. It buzzed beneath her touch—Sally, to tell her that Frank Conrod was on his way down to see her...

'Ah, Dominique, looking as attractive as ever,' Frank Conrod said genially, using the identical words he had before—was it only a week ago?—as he once again lowered his bulk into her chair. 'Congratulations, my dear!'

Dominique blinked. 'I don't quite understand.'

'I've just been speaking to Rory Jones. He was most impressed, Dominique, most impressed. He also told me that following your summing up of the situation and your expert advice he's decided to form a holding company to gather together the threads of the Jones empire, the family trusts, the other interests et cetera.'

Frank Conrod beamed delightedly at Dominique. 'He's offered *me* a position on the board—all thanks to you, my dear. I can tell you confidentially that I would have expected him to do this for Lancelot, but it came as something of a surprise—well, perhaps I need say no more. And, in recognition of your contribution, we at Conrod, Whitney & Smith have decided to offer you a junior partnership.'

Champagne— Oh, Dominique,' Sally said softly. She'd rushed in just after Frank Conrod had left, obviously having been made party to the news, only to discover her boss weeping bitterly into her hands. 'Tell me, love. Here.' And she handed over her handkerchief tenderly.

'He was just…impossibly nice,' Dominique wept. 'I should hate him, and sometimes I did and do, but even while I know I can't ever have him…I don't really hate him at all.'

'Emory Jones?' Sally said quietly. 'It really happened for you with him?'

'It really happened for me, not for him.' Dominique mopped her eyes and blew her nose. 'And now, thanks to him, I've got a junior partnership even though he thinks Frank Conrod is an old woman. Wouldn't you call that nice?'

Sally sighed. 'You poor kid.' And she put her arms around Dominique. 'So he's one of those loners who can't be pinned down?'

Dominique lifted her head and stared at her. 'How did you know?'

'He sort of had it written all over him.' Sally shrugged.

Dominique closed her eyes. 'Well, he certainly can't be pinned down by me. Not for anything permanent like marriage. Perhaps only one woman could have done that, but even she failed.'

'Maybe you should think that the failure's on his side?'

'Why? Because *two* failures are a bit hard to take, even for me?' Dominique asked with irony.

'No, of course not,' Sally said briskly. 'That's utter nonsense, and we both know it. Now look here, kid, I may only be your secretary but I can tell you this: not many girls are as bright and beautiful as you are, so stop selling yourself short!' And she gazed at Dominique sternly. 'If you've at last got a vision in your heart of what you want from a man, what you deserve, then you go for it and nothing less.'

'It's funny you should say that,' Dominique said slowly. 'That's what he said to me.'

'And if nothing else comes of it at least he's cured you of Bryce Denver, by the look of it!'

Dominique sniffed and grimaced. 'He certainly did that. Oh, well, it's back to work, I guess.'

The phone rang. 'Shall I say you're in or out?' Sally asked.

'Uh...in.' Dominique sat forward. 'Unless it's Bryce—I'm permanently out to him. Oh, and if it's Gayle Gyngell would you tell her I'm back but in conference all day?'

It was Gayle Gyngell who came to see her that night.

'Gayle!' Dominique opened the door wider to admit her diminutive friend with a rueful look. 'Sorry I couldn't return your calls but—'

'You were away!' Gayle waltzed in wearing one of her own creations—a cobalt-blue, halter-necked trouser suit.

At a tick over five feet, even in platform shoes, and with her hair dyed platinum, daisy earrings as big as the real thing and blue lipstick and nail varnish, Gayle

Gyngell took your breath away—but not only because of her outward appearance. She also radiated vitality.

'See you took me at my word—my word about Rory Jones, Dom, darling. You went away with him for a whole week! That's more than I managed—and a lot of others, I can tell you. But tell me all about it! And if you could offer me a cuppa at the same time I'd be doubly grateful. I'm pooped, what with these fashion awards coming up!'

But Dominique had herself well in hand, she discovered. 'There's not a lot to tell; it was business.'

'Uh-huh! What's this?'

Dominique bit her lip as Gayle rifled through four items of apparel that she'd happened to have over her arm when she'd opened the door.

'Wow!' Gayle continued. 'Pretty sexy bikini, but not your style, I would have thought. And glory be! What a gorgeous nightgown—what is this, Dom? You breaking out or something? I like the dress too, despite the fact there's not one Gayle Gyngell label in sight.'

'Come into the kitchen and I'll put the kettle on,' Dominique said firmly, wrestling the clothes from her friend and chucking them onto her bed as they passed the bedroom door. 'I'm just sorting my laundry out.'

'So,' Gayle said in quieter tones as they took their tea into the lounge, 'did business with Rory Jones come up to your expectations? Did you get to meet any of his family on this "trip to the hinterland", as your secretary put it?'

'Yes, I met Belinda and her husband, Luke, who broke his arm while I was there, poor bloke. And his cousin Bernard.'

'Who married Anna Bascombe,' Gayle said quietly.

'Look, it wasn't until after you'd gone that I suddenly remembered I'd told Belinda about you and that bastard Bryce Denver, but it happened—'

'It's all right.' Dominique smiled wryly at her. 'She told me how it happened.'

'Did you meet Anna Bascombe that was?'

'Yes, I did, as a matter of fact,' Dominique contrived to say casually. 'She's very attractive.'

'Some say she's the only woman Rory Jones loved,' Gayle said slowly, but her eyes were intent on Dominique's face.

'Do they? They could be right, for all I know—you didn't tell me that when we were discussing him, incidentally.'

'I didn't say *I* believed it; it was quite a long time ago, and to be perfectly honest I didn't want to frighten you off any more than you already were, but—I know Anna,' Gayle said unexpectedly. 'She used to model. She was very ambitious.'

Dominique stood up suddenly. 'She and Bernard have two children now.'

'Do you think she pulled the wrong rein?'

'Gay...it's got nothing to do with me—'

'Belinda does, and she reckons it's still killing her.'

Dominique stopped and narrowed her eyes. 'Have you been in touch with Belinda recently, Gay?'

'Yes. Yesterday. But she got in touch with me; she and Luke are here on the coast for him to recuperate and she got in touch—to discuss you. To tell me she thinks you're the only woman Rory has been serious about since Anna.'

The silence stretched between them, then Dominique shrugged and said abruptly, 'She's wrong. I don't know what happened between them but he's not serious about me. Gay, will you do me a favour—will you just leave it?'

'But *I* do know what happened between them, Dom. I may be one of the very few who does.'

'Look, I don't want to hear it; it's not going to make any difference anyway—' She stopped and bit her lip.

Gayle sat back and said quietly, 'I thought so. I've only seen you look like this twice in your life—when your parents died and when Bryce decamped.'

'*How* do I look?' Dominique demanded. 'You're making me feel like some kind of freak, Gay!'

'No—it's only because I know you so well and I can tell when your nerves are stretched almost beyond endurance.'

'Well, giving me all Rory Jones's secrets isn't going to help in the slightest,' Dominique said shortly.

'But it might make you understand at least. I knew Anna when she was nineteen; that's when I first met her. She was gorgeous—that kind of drop-dead gorgeousness you don't often see—but raw, although even then... Well, perhaps the kindest way you could say it is that she had a "patron".'

Dominique stared. 'A man?'

'A married man,' Gayle said.

'But...why?' Dominique said stupidly. 'I mean, she's so cultured, so... Are you telling me she was a prostitute or a nymphomaniac or something like that?'

'No, I'm not, exactly,' Gayle said. 'I'm telling you she clawed her way up from a very poor background by any means she could—she used her beauty and her body and her brains. And don't think she's in any way unique—many girls do so, and when you see the way men fall for them, well, you can't help thinking there's a sort of quid pro quo about it.'

Dominique swallowed.

'But she was very discreet about it and she was a *very* quick learner. Then she met Rory—only, for reasons best known to himself, the Jones family empire didn't get mentioned. He'd fallen out with his father anyway at the time and he was concentrating on building up his landscape-gardening firm; they were doing a big project here on the coast—a hotel with extensive grounds—and he was in there, boots and all—'

'Hang on,' Dominique interrupted. 'How *do* you know all this? Or are you simply theorising?'

Gayle grimaced. 'No. I put the bits I know together with the bits Belinda knows. It's got to be right.'

'Go on,' Dominique said with a frown.

'Well, unbeknownst to Rory, Bernard Graham lobbed on the scene, became instantly smitten with Anna Bascombe, who failed to make the connection—I told you anyway what a discreet mob they all are, although Bernard obviously didn't fail to make a *wealthy* impression, so to speak—and to cut a long story short when he offered marriage Anna accepted. Rory had apparently not got to that point—or had refused to be blackmailed into marriage. You can imagine his frame of mind when he discovered *who* the other man was, however.'

'How could...she do that?' Dominique whispered.

'To give her her due, she was one of eight children raised on a dirt farm with a drunken father who wasn't above beating the living daylights out of her.'

'I would never have believed it,' Dominique said helplessly.

'No,' Gayle said soberly. 'You have to give her full marks for something.'

'And yet there was, well, a little spark of something

in her that I couldn't quite understand—oh, and something else makes sense now.'

'What?'

'Although *she* brought your name up, she looked rather...odd.'

'Yes, I think I'm one of the very few people who knows this, but, believe it or not, I've never told a soul.'

Dominique looked at her wryly.

'Well—' Gayle shrugged '—you see all sorts of things in my trade and you do get to know about quid pro quos. In some respects I can't help admiring her.'

'And Rory didn't try to stop the wedding?'

'Now, that I don't know—you're on your own from here on in, Dom!'

Dominique stood up restlessly. 'With nowhere to go. No, Gay. Look, I appreciate...that you're trying to help but...it's over.' She wiped her eyes briefly with her hand. 'Believe me.'

And for once in her life Gayle Gyngell sat back and decided that discretion might be the better part of valour. 'OK. Look, are you coming to the fashion awards? It's four weeks tonight—I've been working on a dress for you to wear—and I could pick up an award. As my oldest friend and supporter—do you remember those dresses we made at school?—I'd love you to be there!'

CHAPTER NINE

A MONTH later Dominique stood in the middle of her living room in Gayle's latest creation and sighed. The last thing she felt like doing was going to the fashion awards; she was tired, she felt that she was thin and pale—the outfit had certainly had to be taken in—and she was certainly not in the right mood to show it off to its best advantage, lovely as it was.

She looked down at the heavy eau-de-Nil lace tunic-top, with a mandarin collar and pearl buttons down the front and a matching, slim, gathered silky crêpe skirt. Gayle had said at the final fitting two days before, 'You do realise you show off my more conservative creations to perfection, don't you, Dom?'

'Thank you. As befitting a conservative, academic type of female?'

'Well, you don't look academic in this,' Gayle had replied through a mouthful of pins. 'You look elegant, classy, mysterious—and all the more so because it's not strapless or backless.'

'I feel like a piece of washed-out laundry, however.'

Gayle had sat back on her heels and observed her friend narrowly. But she'd made no reference to Rory Jones in the last weeks and didn't do so now. 'Why don't you take a day off work and splurge in the beauty parlour the day after tomorrow? Have the lot! A massage, a manicure—just let yourself be pampered!'

Dominique had grimaced wryly but she had taken

168

half a day off this afternoon and had attempted to pamper herself.

She'd gone to the hairdresser and had her hair cut to shoulder length and put up in a loose, stylish knot. She'd stopped on the way home from work and bought some new cosmetics and some relaxing herbal bath salts. She'd also treated herself to a new set of underwear, and had been able to find an eau-de-Nil set that matched her outfit, and bought herself a bunch of roses.

Once home, she'd done her nails carefully, she'd soaked in the bath and applied cotton-wool pads soaked in another herbal remedy to her eyes. She'd moisturised her whole body and dressed with care, smoothing the finest stockings onto her legs.

And here I am now, she thought—perfumed, powdered, groomed to within an inch of my life and wishing I didn't have to go to this... If it wasn't Gayle I wouldn't. I just hope she hasn't conjured up a man for me.

The awards were being held in the ballroom of the Marriott Hotel, and it took her a while to find parking in the basement garage; that, together with her reluctance to leave home, saw her arriving a bit late.

She handed in her ticket and was being guided toward Gayle's table when she stopped dead in her tracks as she saw who was sitting next to Gayle with the only empty space at the table beside him: Rory. In a black dinner suit, impeccable white shirt and bow-tie and looking more handsome than she'd ever seen him—and very much at home.

She dug her fingernails into her bag, closed her eyes briefly and wondered how she could escape, but it was too late... Everyone at the table turned towards her expectantly, Rory stood up—and Gayle leapt into action.

'Dom, I thought you were going to desert me! Now, who haven't you met? Doesn't she look stunning?' she said to the table at large. 'I must tell you it's one of my own!'

'Dominique,' Rory said quietly, and pulled out her chair, 'don't faint.'

'I'm not going to,' she said unsteadily, but knew that she probably looked unnaturally pale. 'Was this your idea or hers?'

But he got no opportunity to reply as Gayle began to make introductions. And only then did she realise that Belinda was at the table too, with Luke, in a dinner jacket draped over his cast, looking uncomfortable beside her.

'Hi, Dominique,' Belinda said. 'You do look stunning!'

'Thank you,' Dominique said mechanically, and sat down dazedly.

'And now, ladies and gentlemen,' the compère said from the stage, 'let us begin! Our first category tonight is sportswear.'

And the lights dimmed, everyone turned expectantly to the stage and Rory said, 'We could get out of here.'

'Why?'

He looked at her ironically, and suddenly Dominique knew that she had to leave under any circumstances, because she felt suffocated, unable to sit still and totally unnerved. 'All right.'

He bent his head and said something to Gayle, who looked swiftly over her shoulder at Dominique then nodded.

There were a few surprised glances and one particularly searching one from Belinda as they left the table, but Rory possessed himself of her hand and led her out with the minimum of fuss.

She reclaimed it as they got into the brightness of the ballroom foyer, saying, 'Thanks. Rory, I think I'd rather go home, alone. If Gayle did this it's probably as embarrassing for you as it is for me—'

'She didn't.'

Her eyes widened as she stared up into his. 'You did? Why?' she whispered.

'I wanted to catch you off guard.'

'Oh...' Dominique put a hand to her face in a sudden little gesture of despair.

'Would you let me take you home, Dominique?'

'No, no...'

'Then I think you'd better let me buy you a drink.' And he took her elbow authoritatively. 'You look as if you're about to collapse again.'

It was unfortunately true, but somehow she got her legs to walk, and when they came to the Café on the Lagoon, set outside on the hotel's river terrace, she stopped and breathed the fresh air deeply and gratefully.

'Will this do?' he said quietly.

'I...'

'Dominique, we're going to talk whether you like it or not.'

She licked her lips. 'Why? Hasn't it all been said?'

'No. Sit down.' And he pulled out a chair for her again and gestured to a waiter. 'What would you like?'

'A...a glass of wine, thank you.' She sank down while he ordered the wine and a beer for himself.

And only when their drinks had arrived did he say, 'I thought you'd be in Malaysia by now—Sarawak or Rawa.'

Dominique sipped her wine in silence, then took a steadying breath. 'I cancelled. I may have to thank you for this—they made me a junior partner, so—'

'I know.'

'So it wasn't a good time to go away,' she said, and stopped. 'Did you...suggest it?'

He grimaced. 'I may have put the germ of the idea into Frank's brain, that's all.'

'Well, thank you. He was very pleased to be invited onto your board.'

'I know that too.' And for an instant that look of wicked amusement she knew well glinted in Rory Jones's eyes.

'I hope he's not too much of a cross to bear,' Dominique murmured. 'But you didn't have to do any of it. I would have survived.'

The glint died and something harder took its place. 'As well as you're surviving on a personal level without me?' he suggested.

'Look, if you've been talking to Gayle...' Dominique said evenly.

'I haven't. Belinda must have, on the other hand. It was she who mentioned this evening and said you'd be attending. It was she who organised a ticket for me.'

'When?'

'This morning. I flew in late last night to see you, but this seemed a good enough way, if not better than any other. And...' he paused '...I can see with my own eyes that it's not going well for you, Dominique.'

'So...' She cleared her throat but went on with difficulty, 'What have you got to offer me this time, Rory? More liberalisation? I have to remind you you told me yourself not to take second best from anyone.'

'No—a proposal of marriage.'

Dominique swallowed and was struck speechless.

A faint smile played on his lips but his eyes were unamused.

'Why?' she whispered at last.

'Because I fell in love with you but I was too…criminally dumb to see what had happened to me.'

'I…don't believe you,' Dominique said hoarsely.

'Why not?' He raised an eyebrow. 'Didn't it happen to you?'

'Yes, well…oh!' She blushed brightly. 'It's not the same thing.'

He sat forward attentively. 'Tell me why.'

'You know why—that was something else you told me: why you would be impossible to be married to. Only—' She swallowed, then whispered, 'I just can't help wondering if it isn't still to do with Anna Bascombe…'

He frowned. 'So you know more about her now. I wonder if you know the right story?'

'I—'

'Never mind. Will you let *me* tell you, Dominique?' And before she could protest he started to, in clipped accents.

She stared at him, her green eyes dazed, when he finished a few minutes later, because in a clinical fashion he'd told her the same story that Gayle had. 'How does that check out?' he finished drily.

'Yes…I mean, it does,' she stammered, 'but—'

'Who told you, Dominique?'

'Gayle… She first knew Anna when she was nineteen, but none of this means to say you'll ever be cured of her, Rory.'

He raised an eyebrow. 'Then why do you think I'm asking you to marry me, Dominique?'

She made a sudden decision. 'I don't know. Nor do I know why you're…almost attacking me like this. But one thing I do know: I'm not putting myself through any more of it. Goodbye, Rory.' And she got up and walked swiftly away.

She took a wrong turning in the hotel lobby, had to backtrack, finally found the right staircase for the basement garage and then, when she got down it, for a moment couldn't remember where she'd parked her car. She sat in it for a couple of minutes gathering her composure, before finally reversing out and driving towards the exit, only to discover when she got there that a Land Rover she recognised was blocking it.

The door opened and Rory got out.

Dominique looked around wildly and incredulously, but he simply walked over to her car, opened the door and said, 'Come with me, Dominique—I'm not letting you run away.'

'But you can't do this!' she protested. 'There must be someone, an attendant—Rory, we're creating a traffic jam,' she added desperately as a car came up behind her.

'I'm not moving until you agree to come with me,' he said quietly, and held his hand out to her. 'And if anyone asks I'll tell them that you love me and would like nothing better than to be my wife, which is all I'm trying to arrange.'

She stared up at him and saw utter determination in his eyes, and another car drove up behind them while the first one tooted.

'Now look here, sir!' An attendant did arrive on the scene at last.

'Ah!' Rory straightened. 'Just what I need—a witness. I'm in fact proposing to this lady,' he said to the attendant.

'Well, sir—' the attendant looked confused '—that's very nice, I'm sure, but—'

'She and I...have been very close, you see—' Rory stopped, but only because the motorist directly behind Dominique had got out of his car and come forward aggressively. Rory said to him, 'Sorry about this, mate, but I'm proposing to this lady and she is—'

'Well, why don't you take her somewhere else to do it?' the man said irritably. 'Funny damn place...' He bent down and looked into Dominique's car and his face changed. 'Miss Lindwall!'

Dominique closed her eyes and groaned inwardly as she recognised a client, and Rory continued gravely, 'That's what I'm attempting to do. She and I have been very close—extremely close, you could say—which is why I'm asking her to marry me, and—'

Then the second motorist, who had left his car unseen, chose to make his presence felt by saying, 'Listen, if you can't take no for an answer, chum—' But he stopped, and they all turned as yet another car drove up.

'Get me out of here, Rory Jones!' Dominique whispered through her teeth.

'Right, come with me,' he murmured, and she was too stunned and embarrassed to resist as he helped her out of the car, switched it off, removed the car key from her keyring and handed it to the attendant with something drawn swiftly from his pocket that looked suspiciously like a hundred-dollar note. He also murmured, 'Look after it for the night, will you? We'll be back in the morning.' And he handed Dominique up into the Land Rover.

*   *   *

He took her to the Sheraton Mirage, to a beautifully
appointed suite with an ocean view, but he said nothing—as she had said nothing on the very short drive—
until he handed her a drink. Then all he said was
'Dominique?' with a wryly lifted eyebrow.

'Well, you've finally got me here,' she remarked,
sipped her drink, then put it down with a snap. 'How
could you? I'm not some chattel you can pick up and
put down. Not to mention making an absolute fool of
me!' And she discovered that she was shaking with
emotion and anger.

'I thought it might be the only way to get you to
listen to me,' he answered evenly.

'Did you decide that *after* you decided to catch me
off guard?'

He looked away briefly, but when he looked back his
eyes were steady and sombre, and he said quietly,
'What *are* we fighting about, Dominique?'

'I'm...' She swallowed, then took a breath. 'I'm
fighting the fact that you can expect me to believe this
is...not pity. You came back, decided I was a bit of a
wreck and—'

'Pity?' he said. 'Oh, no. I'm the one to be pitied, if
anything. Look, can I tell you what I've done in the
past month?'

Their gazes clashed; they were only standing a foot
apart and he put his own drink down, but she said
tensely, 'Don't touch me, Rory,' and swallowed.

'All right. Why don't you sit down?'

She looked away with an effort, and walked over to
a couch. He remained standing, looking tall and austere
and unbelievably attractive in his beautifully tailored
dinner suit, and he studied her in silence for a long

moment before he said at last, 'I've resolved the problem of Anna finally.'

Dominique closed her eyes and said wearily, 'How?'

'I've bought Bernard out.'

Dominique's lashes fluttered up and she looked at him incredulously. 'Totally? That must have cost a fortune!'

He grimaced. 'I sold the gold mine to do it, which made us all a bit of money, and with the profits I was able to buy every share he owned in every family enterprise—to his satisfaction. They've left Waverley Downs and are starting a new life somewhere else. It was what he wanted too,' he said sombrely.

'And Anna?'

'I think even Anna realised it was over at last,' he said grimly, 'although some of the true colours showed in the process. But I have to bear a large part of the blame for the fact that it all…went on for so long.

'You see, I've lived the last few years of my life as a living taunt, I suppose you could say—taunting her with the fact that she *could* have had the man she fell in love with, as well as everything Bernard could bring her if not more… But I think even she came to understand what I should have understood a long time ago—that it's simply a matter of indifference to me now, that I see her as a hard, calculating woman, whether by design or circumstance, who will never change.

'Dominique…' He picked up his drink again, with his mouth set, then went on, 'You're probably wondering why I didn't see it ages ago, why I let it drag on for so long—and, of course, I did to an extent; I always knew she was no saint, but there was a fatal fascination about Anna—she was such a mixture of…good and bad. You never knew whether it was love or hate you were experiencing or, for that matter, what she was experiencing. I do know now, though, that I just don't care—except for one thing.'

'What's that?' Dominique said huskily.

He stared at her upswept hair, her perfect make-up, the conservative style, yet rich lace of her beautiful outfit, the soft eau de Nil colour that complemented her green eyes. 'The error it all led me into making with you, my dear,' he said very quietly.

Dominique clasped her glass in both hands and felt her heart beat erratically. But a lonely, bitter month forced her to give nothing away. 'Not such an error, perhaps—at the last moment I don't think you really wanted to sleep with me after all—'

'Oh, yes, I did. And there was an error,' he contradicted her. 'Let me tell you about it.' He bent his head, then looked up with bleak shadows in his blue eyes. 'Yes, I did at one stage convince myself—no doubt prompted by an ego-trip brought on by your lack of response after that first night—that what I was doing to you was therapeutic.

'You were so beautiful, so desirable, and so confused I…told myself it was a criminal waste for you to stay that way. But—' He held up a hand as her eyes registered a flash of hurt that she couldn't control. 'No, let me finish,' he said gently. 'Once I got you to Mount Livingstone and learnt a bit more about you it became much less of an exercise in damage control and much more one with a real sense of concern, and that, I now realise, was when I started to fall in love with you.'

'So you took me away,' she whispered. 'But no sooner did you do that than your conscience started to trouble you, Rory. Is that what you're going to say? I *know* that, and I've had weeks to wonder whether it wasn't because it was a backlash against Anna, taking me away at all.'

'It wasn't—it certainly wasn't because I wanted Anna or because I couldn't have had her at the lift of a finger. It was you—a living torment I couldn't rid myself of. But when I got you to Noosa, Dominique, when I knew you'd decided to take the plunge—yes, my conscience did play up then, because it had become such a habit with me to be a loner it had almost become ingrained. That's what made me hesitate and hold back—a crippling lack of any confidence in my ability to give you more than the...shell of a man I seemed to have become.'

Her lips parted and she stared at him, stunned.

He smiled, but with harsh self-mockery. 'And then it got worse; I could only see that I'd have to hurt you sooner or later, and in my insanity it seemed to me that the least hurtful way would be to do it sooner—that's why I let you, a girl I could slay dragons for, walk away from me.

'That's the error Anna forced me into, Dominique, because that's the legacy I thought she'd left me with for ever. And I didn't understand at the time that I was allowing it to be perpetuated by her always being there, feeding the self-revulsion, did she but know it, and, more importantly, the cynical view I had of myself and my inability to love a woman properly. I didn't understand, that is, until I let you leave me, forced you to leave me. And then I came to see that you were the only one I was going to be lonely without for the rest of my life, that I was going to want you in a way that tortured me and gave me no...peace, that nothing I did with my life was going to make me forget you. But when it did start to become clear to me that's when I took steps to sort my life out so I could come back to you with credibility—if you still wanted me.'

'Rory…' Dominique realised that she had sudden, silent tears streaming down her face. 'Rory,' she tried again, 'but why me? I've thought… I'm a walking disaster where men are concerned, and I *am* a mass of complexes, on top of being an accountant, and we both know—'

'You could always bring your passion for… thoroughness into all your dealings with me, Dominique,' he said gently. 'So far as being a walking disaster—that's what both our lives will be if you don't marry me. Because I'm certainly a disaster area as it is, without you.

'Do you know why, for example, I wanted to catch you off guard? So I could see for myself whether you still loved me. And do you know why I was in that kind of attacking mood? In case I couldn't get you to believe this, that's why.'

'Oh…'

He came over to the couch at last. 'Can I sit down? Not to touch, if you don't want me to, but…?' His eyes questioned hers.

'Yes,' she breathed.

He sat down. 'Do you?' he said barely audibly.

'Still love you?' she whispered, and smiled for a moment as if her heart was breaking. 'I should have thought it was obvious, Rory.'

He said something inaudible, then, 'Do you think you could see your way to lifting the no-touching ban, then, Dominique?' His blue eyes were gentle, yet there was no mistaking the relief in them. 'I know I probably don't deserve it for being such a bloody fool, but I'm going mad by degrees and I need your help.'

She put out a hand and put the back of it to his cheek. 'I never could help myself where you're concerned, Rory.'

He got rid of both their glasses and swept her into his arms.

'Gayle Gyngell,' he said presently, after he'd picked her up and carried her to the bedroom and as he began to undo the pearl buttons of her top. 'At last I've got you in one of her creations—did she design the underwear as well?'

'No, I just happened to find it.'

He opened the tunic wide, and in a sudden, convulsive movement buried his head between her breasts.

'Rory,' she breathed as she stroked his hair, 'it's all right.'

He lifted his head. 'And Poison—you're wearing it again.' He kissed her throat and slid his hands beneath the tunic around her waist. 'There are some of the things I couldn't get out of my mind: the perfume of your skin even when you're not wearing any, the places where your skin is like satin and velvet—these.' He undid her bra and exposed her nipples. Then he withdrew his hands and turned his attention to her hair, removing the pins and releasing it into a tumbled, gold-streaked mass. 'The lovely, dishevelled way you look just before and after love.'

'Dominique?'

She stirred in his arms. 'Yes, Rory?'

'Do you believe me now?'

It was very quiet apart from the sound of the sea, and the first faint tinge of dawn was lightening the sky. They'd slept after making love and their heads were on the same pillow, and beneath the sheet their bodies were still entwined. 'I think I might have to,' she said softly.

'Why is that—I mean, as opposed to wanting to?'

'Well—' she drew her fingers down his arm '—I'm at a certain disadvantage.'

'What's that?'

'I have no clothes other than those I arrived in, which are not particularly appropriate for getting around in during the day.'

'I see—I hadn't thought of that,' he said gravely. 'Now you've put me in mind of it, though, I like the thought of it very much.'

'Having me here as a prisoner of some kind?' she suggested.

'Of love? Definitely. Not that I imagine for one minute that you would stand for it, only you did bring the subject up yourself, so... Well, I can dream a bit, can't I?' he said ruefully, and smiled into her eyes.

She caught her breath and felt herself melting as his body hardened against hers. 'Would you tell me something, Rory?' she said huskily. 'I'm still a little... I still wonder why me?'

'Because you aroused me that first night, Dominique,' he said, 'and never stopped. Because you can be serious and clever at the same time as being astonishingly beautiful and virtuous—which is a combination that intrigues and fascinates me and always will. You never bore me, and you can trade insults with me—yet I know you're one of the nicest people I'll ever meet—and you make love to me in a way that makes *me* feel...like a knight in shining armour, like a king. It's as simple as that.'

'Do I?'

'Would you like me to demonstrate?'

'In a moment. Can I tell you what I love about you?'

He held her closer suddenly, and said not quite evenly, 'Of course.'

'You make me feel as if the rest of my life was coloured grey before I met you; you make me feel alive—' she stroked his face '—adventurous, incredibly attracted to you, adoring, safe, and for some reason—well, quite hopelessly in love with you. So much so that I can't even look at your hands, which are beautiful, or hear your voice sometimes without getting goose-bumps.'

'These hands?' he said barely audibly, and drew them down her body.

'Yes,' she said with a tremor in her voice. 'They're the first thing I—fell for—Rory,' she said on an indrawn breath.

'Sorry,' he murmured. 'I got carried away.'

'I don't mind,' she whispered. 'Do you believe I believe you now?'

'Yes, although I must warn you I won't be happy until I've got a wedding ring on your finger. Dominique—what I said about feeling like a king earlier?'

'Yes?'

'As a matter of fact, right now I feel like a rather lowly knave—a bit helpless and overcome with love, anyway.'

'Well, I think we could soon change that,' she said softly. 'You know, I used to think of you as a tiger, stalking me through the jungle of love—I think you'll always be my very own tiger, although the jungle has become a beautiful garden now— There,' she said lovingly, 'what did I tell you?'

She married him three days later, at a simple ceremony with only Belinda and Luke, Gayle and Sally Henderson present. She wore the pearl-coloured silk dress he'd bought her and carried a bouquet of white rosebuds, and even her friend Gayle Gyngell forgave her for wearing a dress she hadn't designed. And after a lunch in the suite at the Mirage they said goodbye to their guests and turned to each other as the doors closed behind them.

'Dominique?' he said quietly.

'Yes, Rory?' she murmured, twisting her wedding ring round her finger, then looking into his eyes with a half-smile at the back of hers. 'Now you've really got me where you want me.'

'At last,' he concurred. 'But you look a little shell-shocked,' he said, his eyes narrowed and acute.

'Do I?' She smiled properly up into his eyes. 'That's only because of what you do to me, and because—I can't believe how happy I feel.'

'Thank God,' he said, and drew her into his arms. 'So long as there are no regrets,' he said against her hair. 'I *love* you.'

'I love you too. I loved getting married to you and I will always love staying married to you, so there are no regrets—well, only one.' She drew away from him slightly and looked around the room with a little imp of mischief in her green eyes.

He followed her gaze, narrowed his own, then looked down at her wickedly. 'Don't tell me, I think I can guess.'

'Can you?' she replied innocently.

'Yes, I can. No room-divider?' he hazarded.

'No room-divider,' she said gravely.

'But a very adequate bed, Mrs Jones. And all sorts of other interesting spots,' he teased.

'If you say so, Mr Jones,' she replied demurely.

'And—' he laced his fingers through hers '—the rest of our lives together to look forward to.'

'Yes, Rory,' she agreed, and raised her mouth for his kiss.

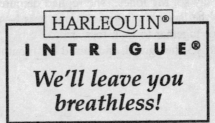

HARLEQUIN®
I N T R I G U E®

We'll leave you breathless!

If you've been looking for thrilling tales of
contemporary passion and sensuous love stories
with taut, edge-of-the-seat suspense—
then you'll *love* **Harlequin Intrigue!**

Every month, you'll meet four new heroes
who are guaranteed to make your spine tingle
and your pulse pound. With them you'll enter
into the exciting world of Harlequin Intrigue—
where your life is on the line
and so is your heart!

THAT'S INTRIGUE—DYNAMIC
ROMANCE AT ITS BEST!

HARLEQUIN®

I N T R I G U E®

HARLEQUIN SUPERROMANCE®

...there's more to the story!

Superromance. A *big* satisfying read about unforget-
table characters. Each month we offer
four very different stories that range from family
drama to adventure and mystery, from highly emo-
tional stories to romantic comedies—and
much more! Stories about people you'll
believe in and care about. Stories too
compelling to put down....

Our authors are among today's *best* romance writ-
ers. You'll find familiar names and
talented newcomers. Many of them are
award winners—and you'll see why!

If you want the biggest and best
in romance fiction, you'll get it
from Superromance!

Available wherever Harlequin books are sold.

Harlequin® Historical

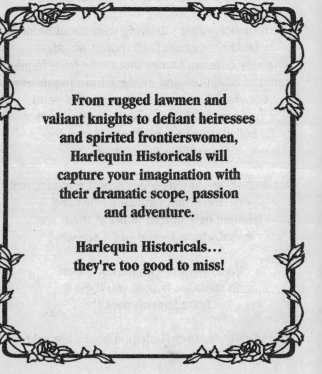

From rugged lawmen and
valiant knights to defiant heiresses
and spirited frontierswomen,
Harlequin Historicals will
capture your imagination with
their dramatic scope, passion
and adventure.

Harlequin Historicals…
they're too good to miss!

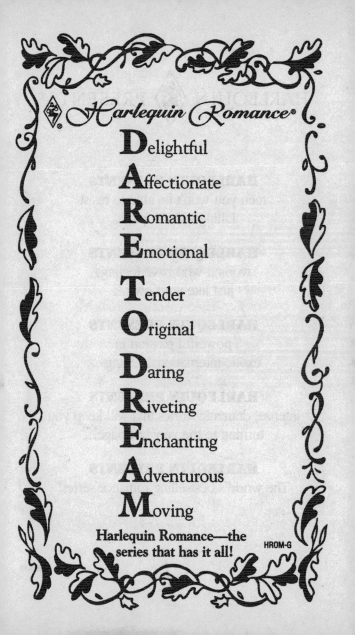

Harlequin Romance®

Delightful

Affectionate

Romantic

Emotional

Tender

Original

Daring

Riveting

Enchanting

Adventurous

Moving

Harlequin Romance—the
series that has it all!

HROM-G

HARLEQUIN PRESENTS®

HARLEQUIN PRESENTS
men you won't be able to resist
falling in love with...

HARLEQUIN PRESENTS
women who have feelings
just like your own...

HARLEQUIN PRESENTS
powerful passion in
exotic international settings...

HARLEQUIN PRESENTS
intense, dramatic stories that will keep you
turning to the very last page...

HARLEQUIN PRESENTS
The world's bestselling romance series!

LOOK FOR OUR FOUR FABULOUS MEN!

Each month some of today's bestselling authors bring
four new fabulous men to Harlequin American Romance.
Whether they're rebel ranchers, millionaire power brokers
or sexy single dads, they're all gallant princes—and
they're all ready to sweep you into lighthearted fantasies
and contemporary fairy tales where anything is possible
and where all your dreams come true!

You don't even have to make a wish...
Harlequin American Romance will grant your every desire!

Look for Harlequin American Romance
wherever Harlequin books are sold!

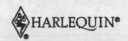 HARLEQUIN®

Not The Same Old Story!

 HARLEQUIN ❖ PRESENTS®

Exciting, glamorous romance stories that take readers around the world.

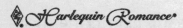 *Harlequin Romance®*

Sparkling, fresh and tender love stories that bring you pure romance.

 HARLEQUIN® *Temptation*

Bold and adventurous—Temptation is strong women, bad boys, great sex!

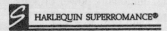 HARLEQUIN SUPERROMANCE®

Provocative and realistic stories that celebrate life and love.

 AMERICAN ROMANCE®

Contemporary fairy tales—where anything is possible and where dreams come true.

 HARLEQUIN® INTRIGUE®

Heart-stopping, suspenseful adventures that combine the best of romance and mystery.

 LOVE & LAUGHTER™

Humorous and romantic stories that capture the lighter side of love.